GUPPY

WILL JAKEMAN'S MARVELLOUS MECHANIMALS
is a GUPPY BOOK

First published in the UK in 2021 by
Guppy Books,
Bracken Hill,
Cotswold Road,
Oxford OX2 9JG

978 1 913101 503

1 3 5 7 9 10 8 6 4 2

Papers used by Guppy Books are from well-managed forests and other responsible sources.

GUPPY PUBLISHING LTD Reg. No. 11565833

A CIP catalogue record for this book is available from the British Library.

Printed and bound in Great Britain by Bell and Bain Ltd

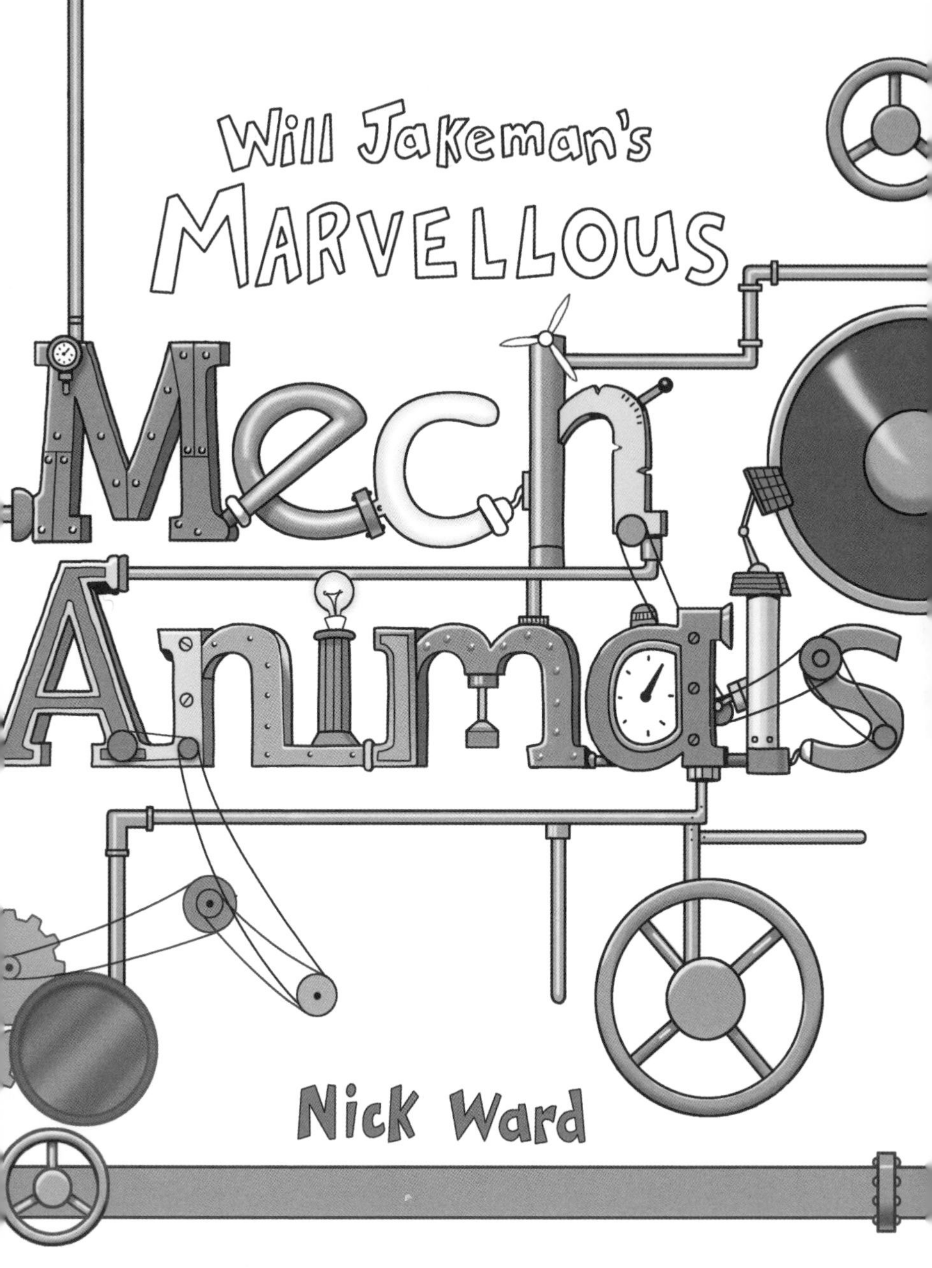

Will Jakeman's Marvellous Mech Animals

Nick Ward

GUPPY
BOOKS

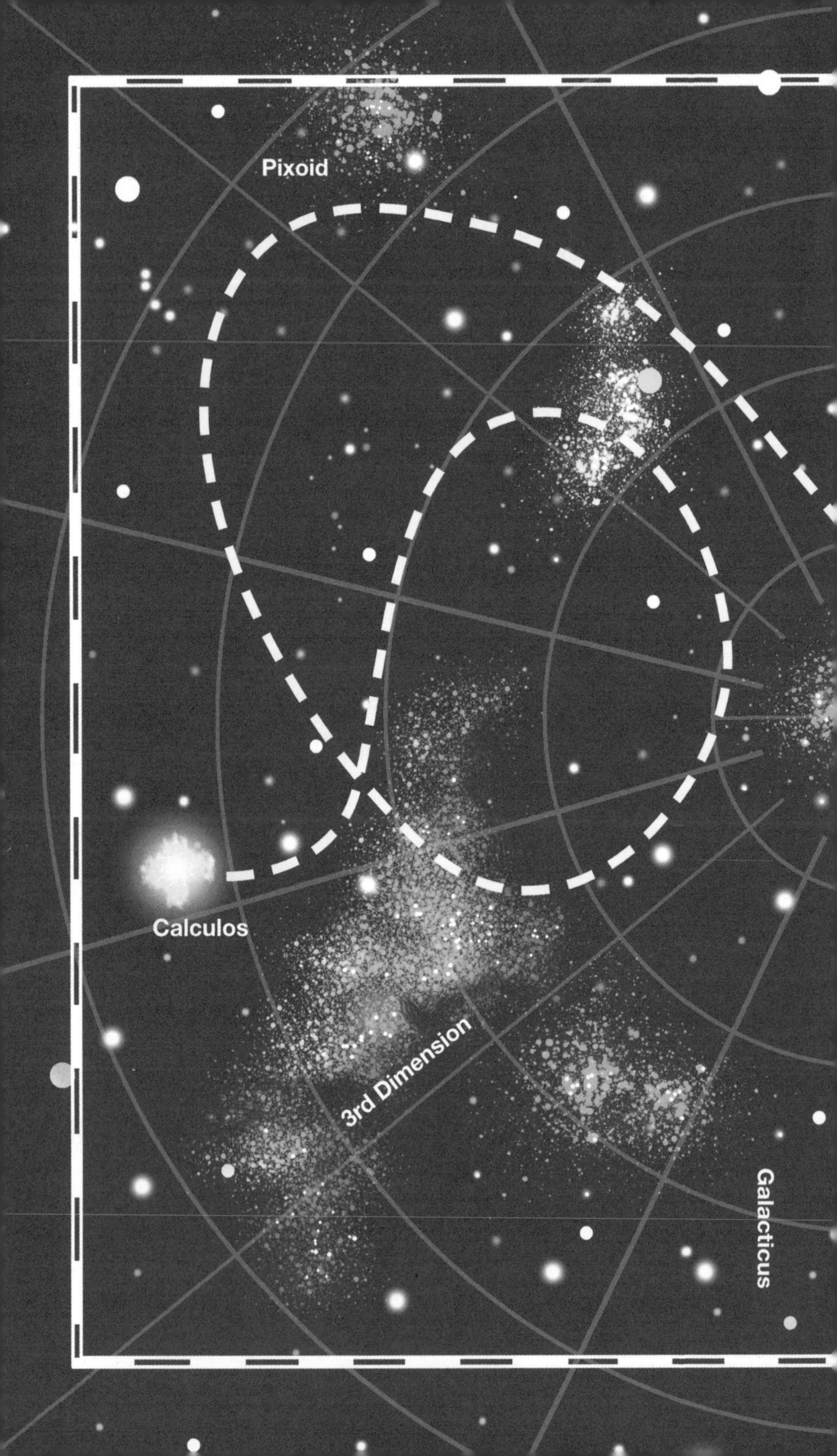

Pixoid

Calculos

3rd Dimension

Galacticus

5th Dimension
Argon
Zapta
Pavos

Greetings, readers!

A Selfie!

Let me introduce myself – my name is Will Jakeman and I'm an inventor, perhaps the best inventor there has ever been. I'm old now, 99½ to be precise, and I'm as wrinkly as a walnut. To look at me, you'd never guess what hair-raising, nerve-jangling adventures I've had. Brilliant adventures, scary adventures, discombobulating adventures! And because I'm old and my memory isn't what it was, I have decided I'd better write everything down before I forget.

My Adventures Begin

I was born in a remote galaxy, beyond the range of the most powerful telescope in existence. One day, when I was a tiny baby, our planet was invaded by an alien army. In a desperate attempt to save me from certain doom, my quick-thinking mum bundled me into an intergalactic i-cot and sent me bobbing down the rushing waters of a nearby river and out onto the storm-tossed sea.

Snug and safe in my little i-cot, I crossed mighty oceans, slipped through hidden portals into other worlds and floated between glittering galaxies. Some time later the i-cot landed in a small, sandy cove on a planet called Urf, where an old couple were out for a morning walk. Eliza and Nat Jakeman were looking for anything useful that had washed ashore in the night, flotsam and jetsam perhaps, but instead they found me!

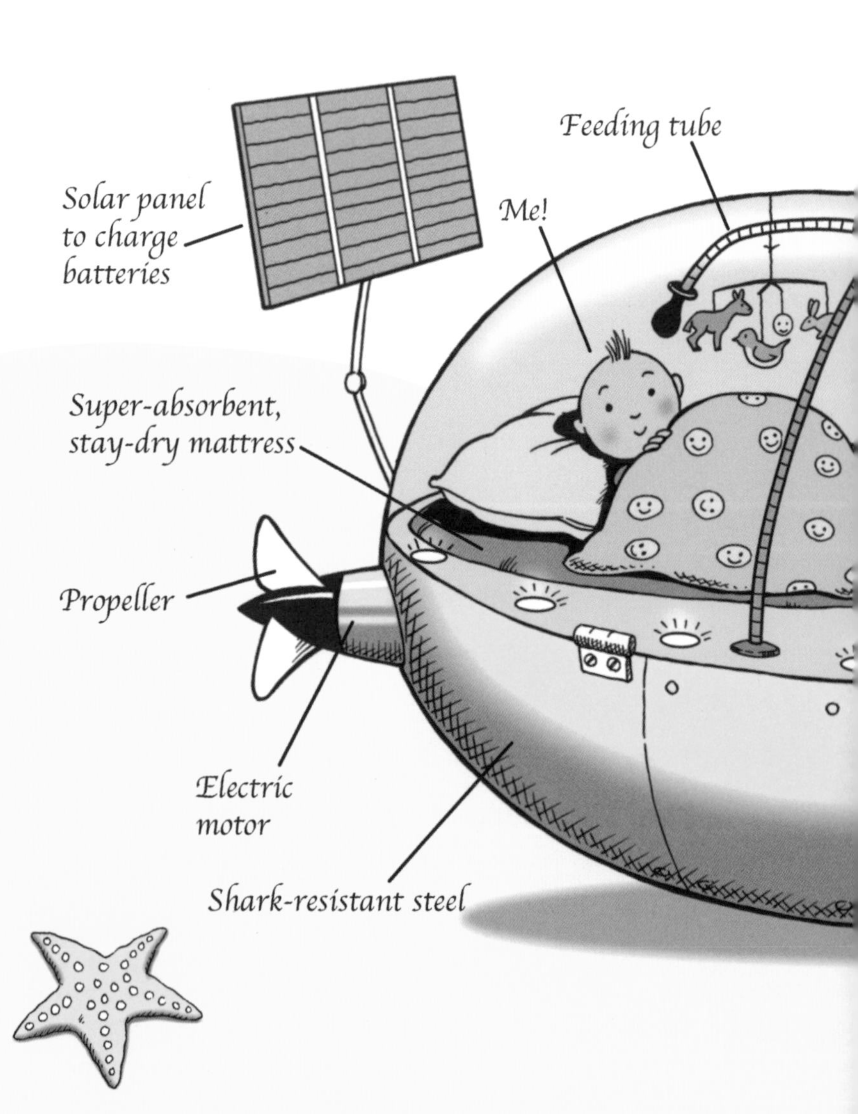

What a shock it must have been, finding a baby bobbing about in a rock pool. Where did I come from? Who did I belong to? What on Urf were they going to do with me?

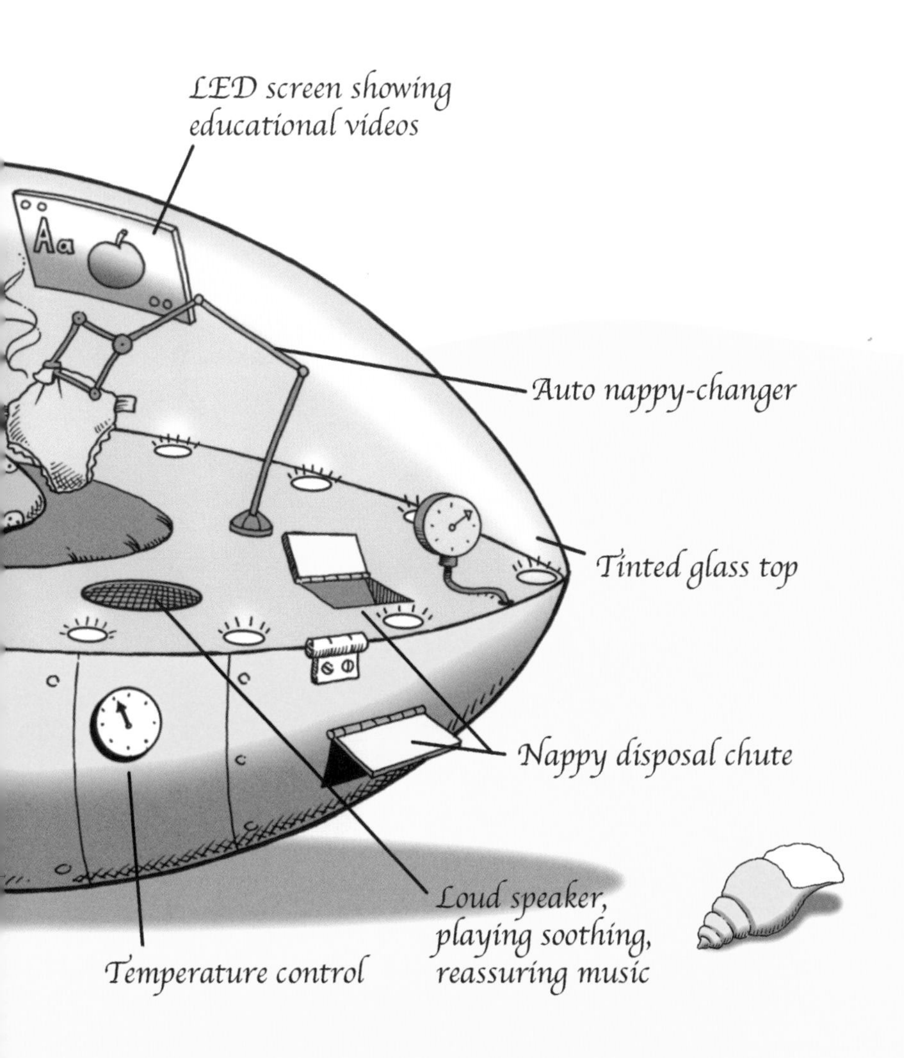

In a daze, the Jakemans rummaged amongst the blankets in my i-cot and found this letter.

HELP!

Our beautiful planet is being attacked by Reptoids, a ferocious gang of interplanetary space pirates. The air is juddering with explosions and buildings are crashing down around us. There is little hope of survival, so I'm sending my precious baby out into the unknown in a special transporter I designed myself. He'll have everything he needs for his journey. His name is Will – please take care of him.

Love from his distraught mum X

The kind old couple immediately decided to raise me as their own son and carried me back to their house – a rambling, dilapidated workshop in the small town near the cove. I always wondered – was it just by chance I ended up being adopted by the Jakemans? Because it turned out the couple were amazing inventors, just like my mother.

My mum

This is the only photo I have of my brave mum. She had just been awarded a prize for inventing.

Eliza Jakeman

An inventor, a mathematician, a scientist and a kind and loving step-mom. When she found me she recognised the baby she had always wanted but never had, and vowed to take care of me.

Nat Jakeman

A wonderful, but rather scatter-brained inventor. The minute he saw my i-cot he took it to bits to see how it worked. I don't think he ever managed to put it back together again!

Of course, I was only a baby when all this happened so I couldn't remember my real home, and I was very happy with my new mom and pop who loved me to bits.

The Jakemans were very well-known inventors. People came from far and wide to buy their wonderful machines: inventions like the bed that turned into a bath without you having to get out of it – a very popular one!

Or the hat that cut your hair in a choice of five different styles while you were wearing it.

The most popular invention, though, was the vacuum cleaner that operated itself, walking around the house on long, bird-like legs and searching out cobwebs to suck up with its patented dust-seeking radar.

I spent my time playing on the oily floor of their workshop, amongst all the cogs and springs and pressure gauges. I was so fascinated by their inventions that Pop built me a splendid hover-potty so I could whizz around the factory and help them with their work. I used to pass them spanners and oilcans and tighten nuts and bolts.

(I loved that potty! Wish I had one now…)

It wasn't too long before I started to have my own ideas, and by the age of six I'd invented my very first machine – the **Breakfast Making Hat**. It was meant to save grown-ups time by cooking their breakfast on the way to work…

I remember Pop was very encouraging, but my invention wasn't a great success. The hat brewed piping hot tea all right, but dripped it down the back of your neck, and the tasty bacon sandwiches caught fire. I realised this inventing lark wasn't as easy as my parents made it look!

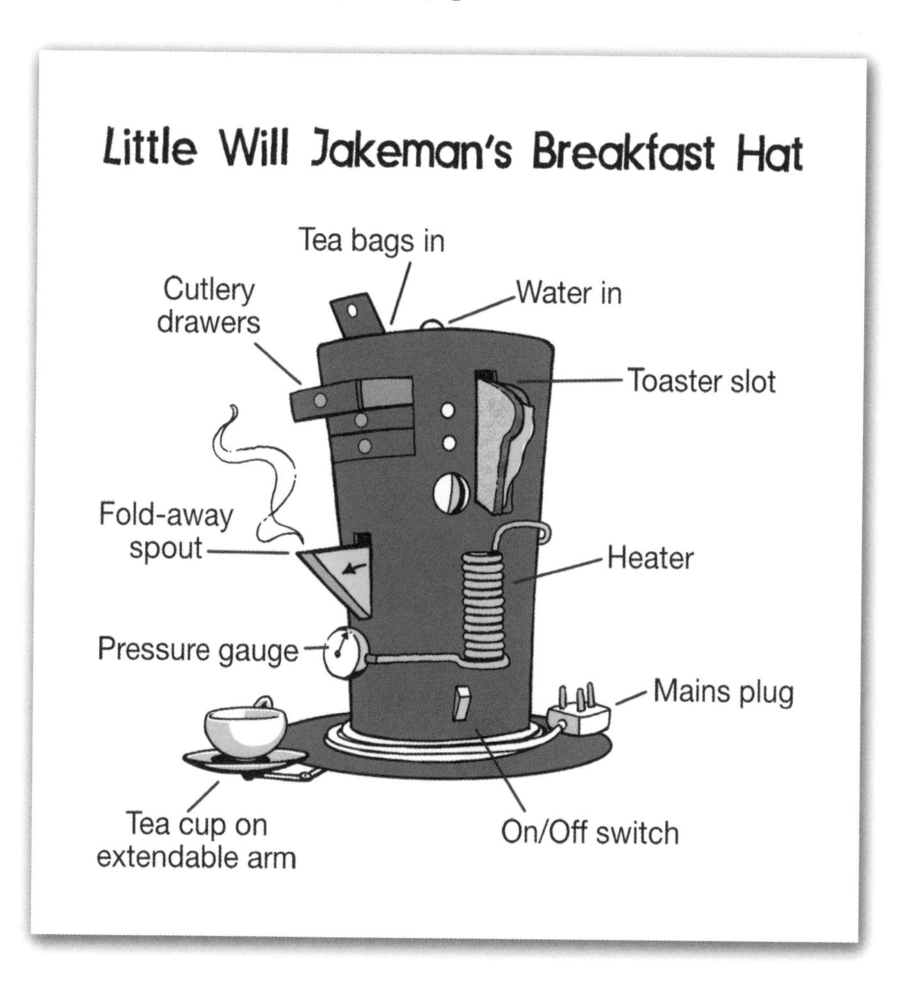

It had given me the inventing bug, though, and from that moment on there was no stopping me. I sketched my ideas into notebooks and before long, with help from Mom and Pop, I had made all sorts of amazing things.

Soaring Raptor Wings

When I was seven I made my own set of wings. They were very low-tech, relying on a string and pulley system, but they worked! I managed to get two metres off the ground and stay airborne for five minutes before I became too exhausted, and had to land.

Snoop!

I wasn't allowed to have a real dog, so I made one instead. He moved by a self-winding clockwork motor, and was guided by a sensor control. Snoop was a true and faithful friend until Mom decided he needed a bath and his cogs got rusty and seized up. No amount of oiling would help, so Snoop is now a doggy ornament!

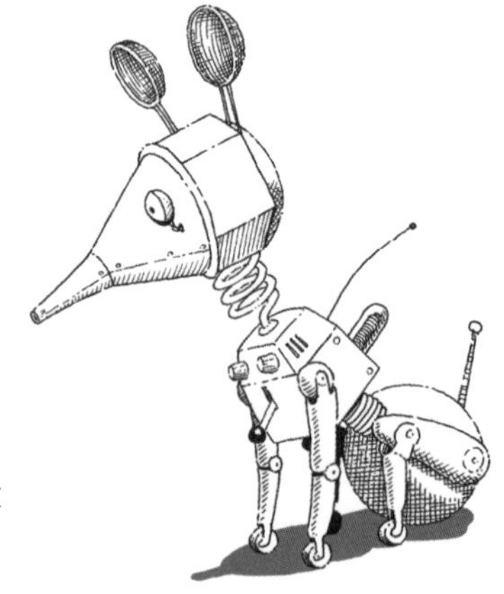

I Become a Proper Inventor

I became better and better at inventing, and it wasn't long before Mom and Pop were struggling to keep up with my creations. I made all sorts of useful things, like everlasting chewing gum and self-propelled roller-skates, but by the time I went

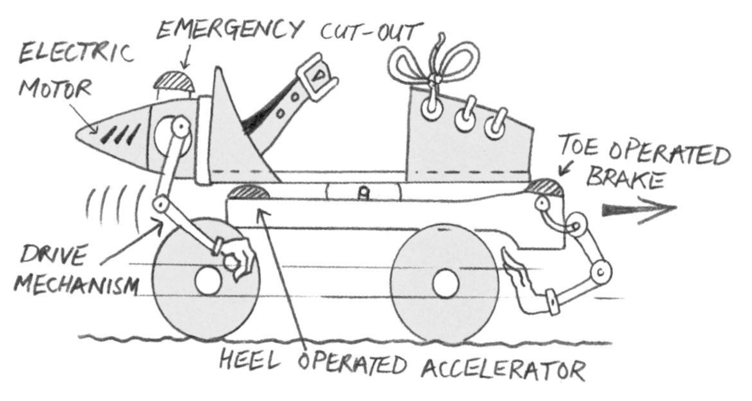

INITIAL SKETCH FOR MOTORISED SKATES

to school I'd found out that what I really needed was a bodyguard…

Urf is home to some very scary creatures that occasionally roam into town looking for an easy meal – like the Horror Hound, a terrifying canine with powerful jaws and a miniscule brain.

Or the Cronies – squat, bouncing balls of blubber with wide, fang-filled mouths and a curved horn on the back of their heads. No one knew where they came from, but they made my walk to school pretty treacherous and I often had to run for my life.

I was also having problems with some of the other children. Some of the bigger boys started calling me names when they saw me scribbling ideas in my notebook. They pushed me as I walked past, and emptied my school bag onto the ground. Even though my best friend, Titch, stuck up for me and told them to leave me alone, it didn't do any good. In fact it made the bullies even worse.

So I decided to do something about it. I invented what became the very first of my world-famous Mechanimals: a robotic, hydrogen-powered metal gorilla. It took a long time to make **Steel-Skull**, but this invention was extra-extraordinary – even if I say so myself!

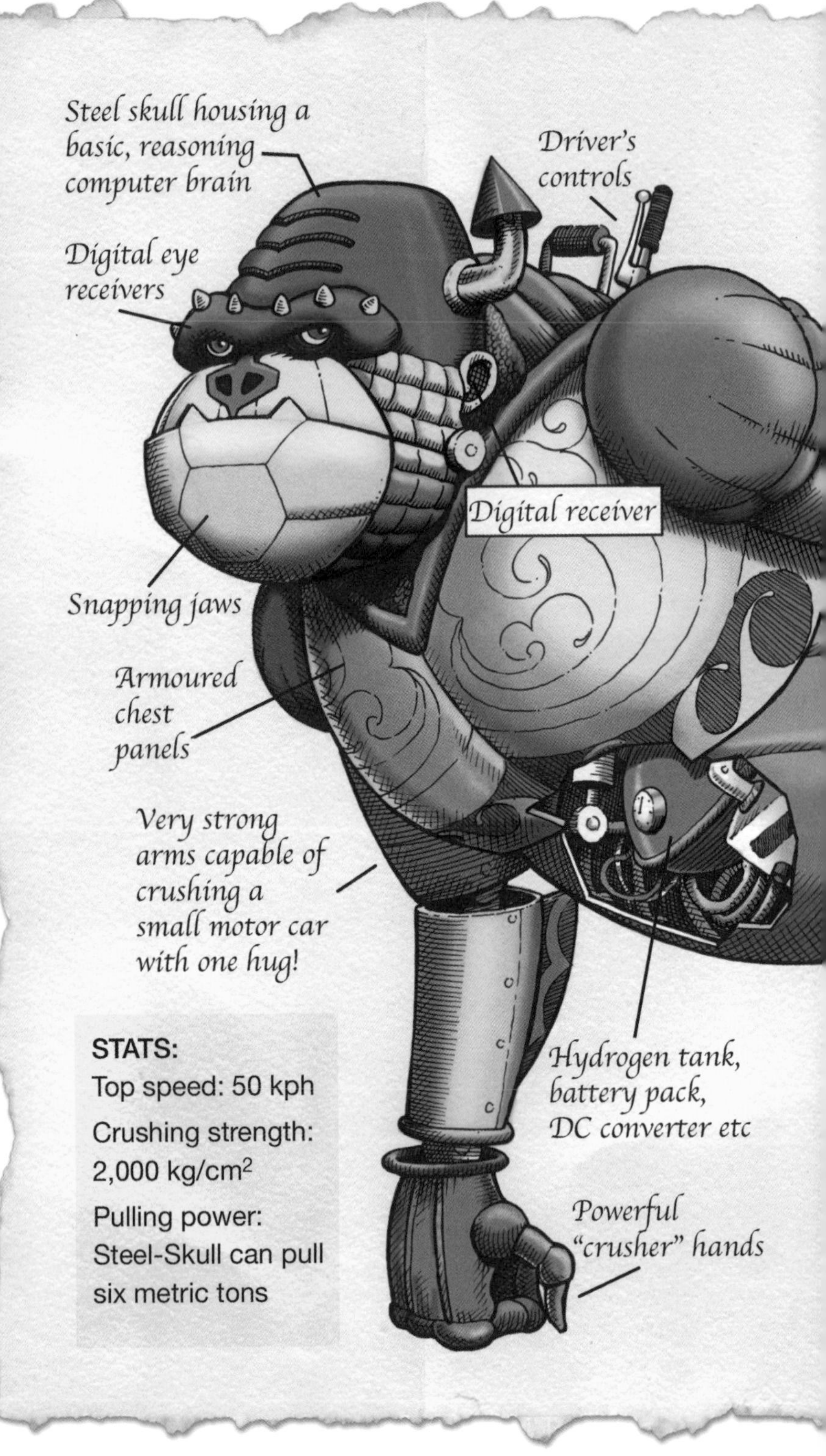

STATS:

Top speed: 50 kph

Crushing strength: 2,000 kg/cm^2

Pulling power: Steel-Skull can pull six metric tons

Steel-Skull

Steel-Skull's hydrogen tank feeds a battery pack that uses hydrogen and oxygen to create electricity that drives pistons and cogs, moving the Mechanimal's arms and legs. Steel-Skull is self-propelled but can also be ridden and controlled from a seat on his shoulders.

Patent No. WJMech0001

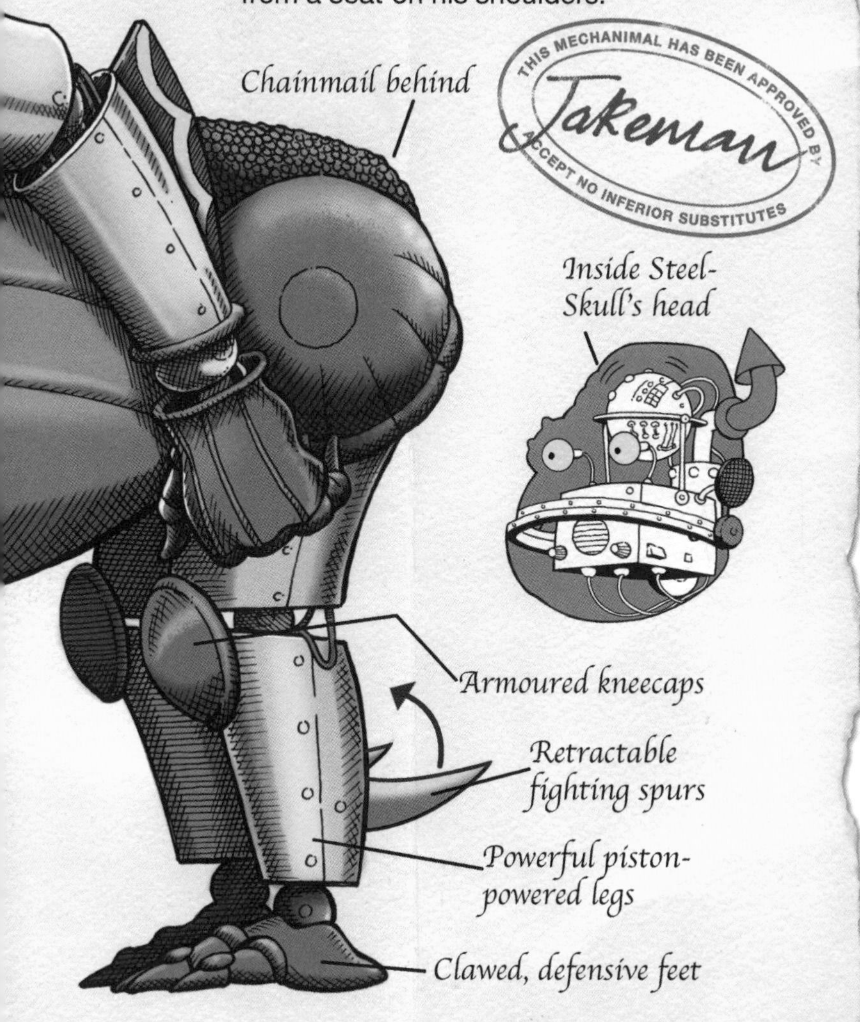

Steel-Skull's hydrogen motor was one hundred percent environmentally friendly, and its only emission was pure, clean water. He was super-strong and would walk beside me on my way to school, his knuckles sparking as they scraped on the pavement.

The Cronies bounced away towards the distant hills when they saw Steel-Skull coming, and the Horror Hound slunk off with its spiked tail between its legs. The school bullies soon changed their ways, too. In fact they became

quite friendly and asked if they could play with him. I didn't mind, and soon my gorilla was giving everyone rides around the playground.

I was so pleased with Steel-Skull, I decided to make more Mechanimals. Mom and Pop continued to lend a hand, but I did most of the work myself.

Soon I'd added the **Armoured Armadillo** to my metal menagerie. It ran on a special fuel invented by Mom and made from fermented rose petals – so the only emissions were a powerful roar and a faint smell of roses. But I'll tell you more about my amazing Armadillo later.

My next Mechanimal was a remote-controlled **Spring-loaded Slithering Snake** that spat fire instead of poison. With the press of a button its electric motor would make the snake's tail wave from side to side, creating a forward thrust that sent the Mechanimal gliding along on the rows of ball bearings set into its undercarriage.

Another button would create a threatening hiss and send a plume of flames shooting from its mouth. It was an absolute cracker, but the remote didn't work properly and I nearly ended up burning our workshop down! After that, Pop made me change it so the snake only spat fake fire made of flickering red and orange lights, but it looked so real I'm sure it would frighten any monster away.

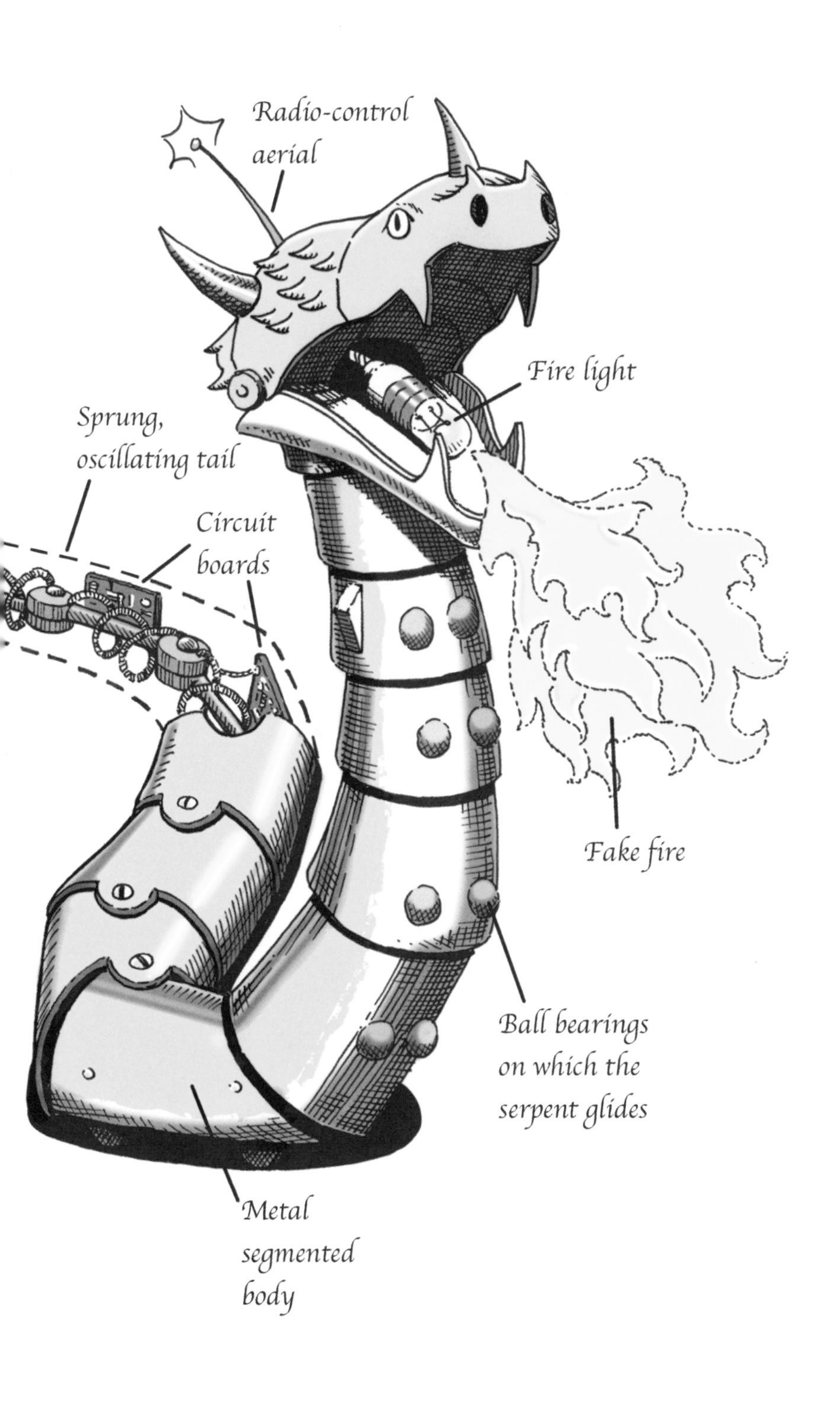
Radio-control aerial
Fire light
Sprung, oscillating tail
Circuit boards
Fake fire
Ball bearings on which the serpent glides
Metal segmented body

Uh-oh! Things Start to go Wrong . . .

I thought nothing could disrupt my happy, carefree life – I loved my mom and pop, I had some great new friends at school and I had a workshop where I could do my inventing. What could possibly go wrong?

When I was nine, Mom and Pop told me my true history; how they found me washed up in Cockle Bay inside the miraculous i-cot. It was a heck of a shock, I can tell you! They showed me the letter my real mum had written, explaining how the world I came from had been invaded by a vast army of marauding Space Pirates.

"I don't believe it!" I said. "You're really saying I don't come from here?"

"That's right, Will," said Mom. "But we love you just as if you were our own."

"So, where do I come from, then?"

"Well, we know it was called Calculos, but that's about all," said Pop. "We've no idea where it is."

He took a large book called *Mythical Marauders of the Universe* from amongst his reference books and opened it.

"Take a look at this, Will," he said.

I stared in horror at a picture of a Space Pirate, and realised how brave my real mother must have been to make sure I escaped their clammy clutches.

The Reptoids

These legendary brigands prowl the oceans that run between time and space in their inter-planetary Air Galleon. They destroy towns, cities and even whole worlds, stealing anything they can lay their slimy hands on.

But I was soon to encounter something just as nasty as a Reptoid Space Pirate, and the danger came from much closer to home…

Just a few weeks later, Mom, Pop and I were busy in the workshop making an automatic page-turning book, when the door suddenly

The Jakeman Auto Page-turner

crashed open. The room seemed to turn chilly and a dark figure stalked in on clattering high heels. It was a tall, thin woman dressed in black from head to foot, with jet black hair piled up in a towering beehive bun and pinned in place with vicious-looking hairpins.

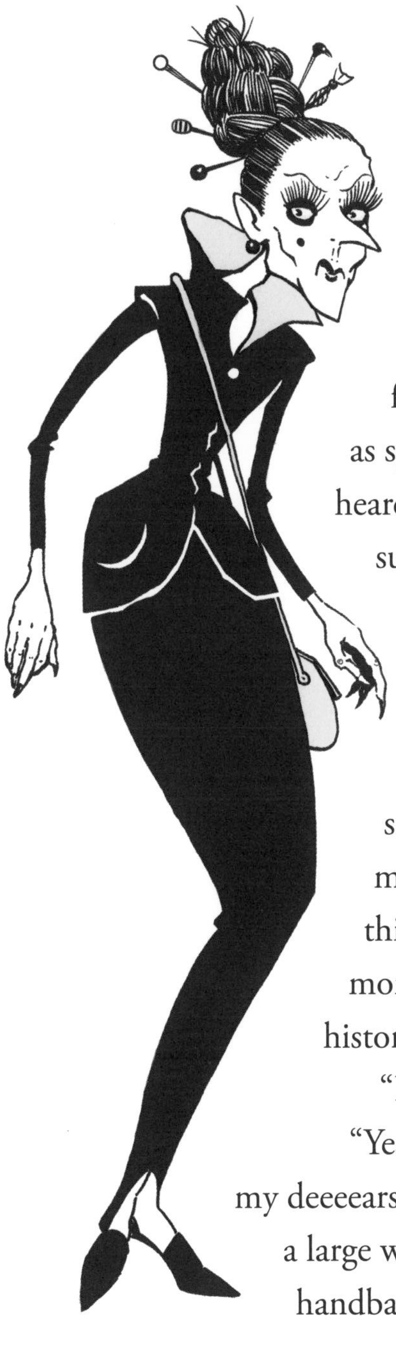

"Can I help you?" asked Pop.

"My name is Ida Gripp," she said in a husky voice, her eyes scanning the workshop from under lashes as long as spider legs. "You may have heard of me – I'm the most successful entrepreneur on Urf. I have heard wonderful things about your inventions, my dears, but it's a strictly small-time operation. With my expertise, I could turn this place into the biggest money-making venture in history. I want to buy it!"

"Buy it?" stuttered Pop.

"Yes – how much will it cost, my deeeears?" And with that she took a large wad of money from her handbag.

"It's not for sale," said Mom, turning back to her work. "Now if you don't mind, we're rather busy..."

"Ah, clever girl – you want to negotiate," said Ida, with a smile. "OK, I'll give you ten thousand more." And she put another pile of notes on the counter top.

"It's not for sale," repeated Mom.

"It will never be for sale," said Pop. "Now please, take your money and leave us in peace."

"Excuse me? You are joking, surely. I'm offering you cold, hard cash," said Ida, her eyes flashing and her voice getting croakier.

"NO!" we all turned round and said together.

"Big mistake!" hissed the extraordinary woman as she stuffed the money back in her bag. "I didn't become the world's most successful entrepreneur by giving up at the first obstacle. I always get what I want in the end – one way or another!"

And with that she turned on her high heels and clomped out of the workshop.

"Strange person," said Pop, continuing

to screw a plug onto the Jakeman Page-turner's gizmo box.

"She gave me the heebie-jeebies," said Mom, with a shiver. "I hope we don't see her again."

But we did see her again. She came back the following week, and the week after that. In fact Ida Gripp came back every week for a month, each time offering us more and more money, and each time we refused. She always began by trying to be as sweet as pie, but grew angrier at every visit. She grew so angry she began to tremble and I thought she might erupt like a volcano!

The whole thing made me feel scared, but Pop told me to put her right out of my mind and carry on as normal. And that's what I tried to do – but no matter how hard I tried or how involved I became with an invention, the memory of Ida Gripp would cloud my thoughts and a shiver would run down my spine.

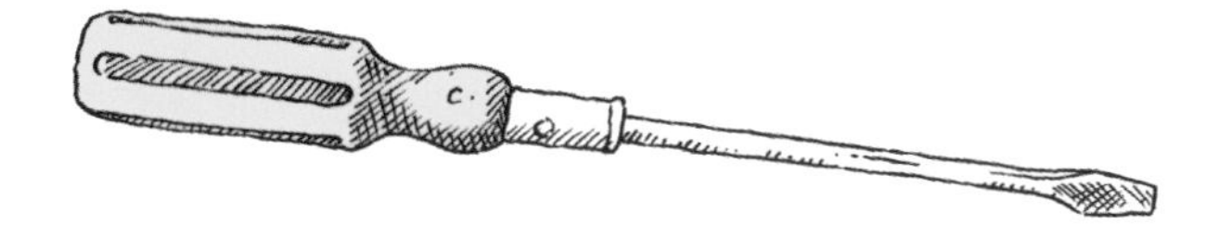

Snatched!

One Saturday, a few weeks later, Titch came over and we went to the park to test my latest invention – a pair of splendid **Compressed-Air Hover Boots**. We were soon putting them through their paces. Titch tried them first, whizzing along a few feet above the ground, then banking into a tight turn and rushing back to where I was waiting for my go.

"They're amazing," said Titch, as I strapped the Hover Boots onto my feet.

"I'll make you a pair, then," I said. "Now watch this!" and I rose vertically in the air until I was level with the treetops.

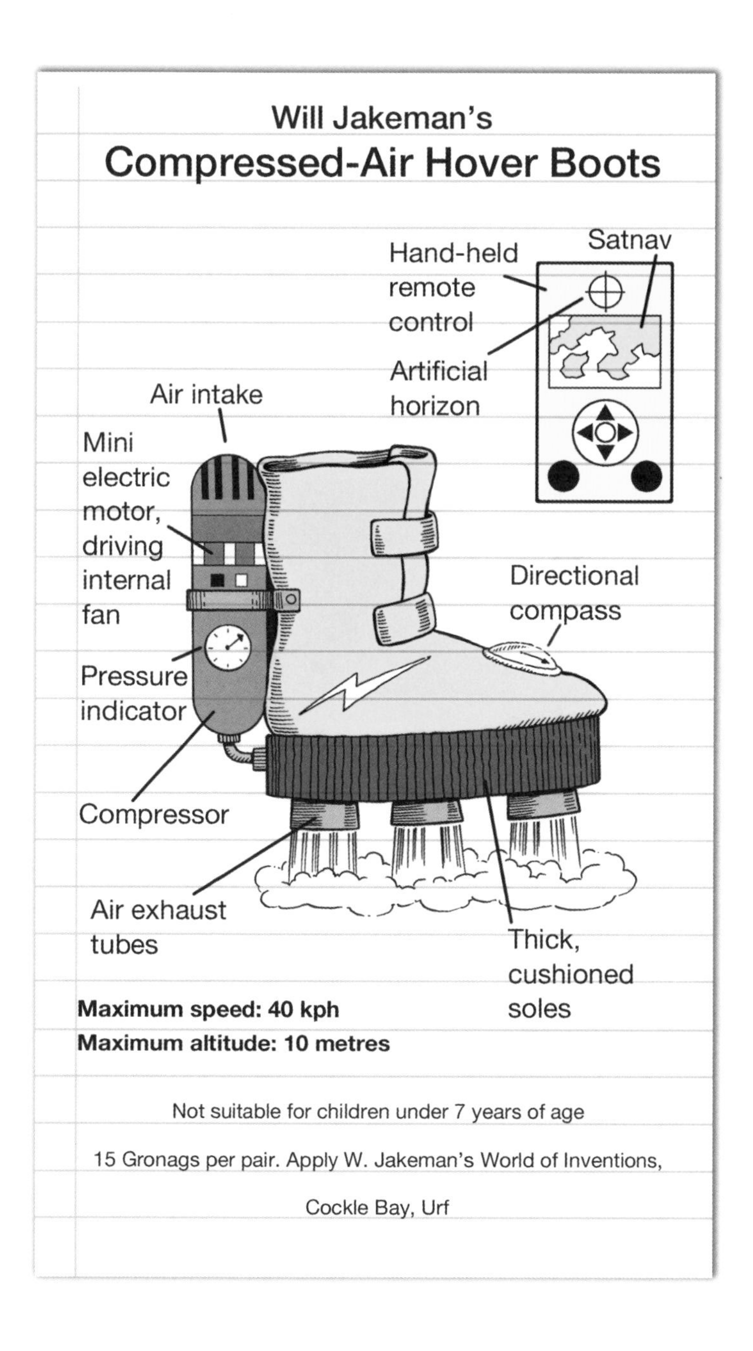
Will Jakeman's
Compressed-Air Hover Boots
Hand-held remote control
Satnav
Artificial horizon
Air intake
Mini electric motor, driving internal fan
Directional compass
Pressure indicator
Compressor
Air exhaust tubes
Thick, cushioned soles
Maximum speed: 40 kph
Maximum altitude: 10 metres
Not suitable for children under 7 years of age
15 Gronags per pair. Apply W. Jakeman's World of Inventions, Cockle Bay, Urf

"Woohoo! I can see for miles," I shouted. But then the sky suddenly grew overcast and the air turned chilly.

"What's happening?" Titch asked, starting to look worried as the sky turned even darker.

"I'm not sure, but I don't like it," I said, with a shiver.

"I think I'd better get home," said Titch.

"Me too. I'll see you at school next week."

Full of dread, I flew home as quickly as my boots could fly me. When I got there I found the workshop doors wide open and the floor littered with scraps of paper and broken machines.

"Mom! Pop! Is anyone home?" I yelled, but there was no reply.

I stood rooted to the spot. What had happened? It looked as if a tornado had whipped through our home. Then I noticed a sheet of paper pinned to the wall by a long, black hairpin, and my heart sank.

"Oh, no," I muttered under my breath as I tore the note down and began to read the spattery, spidery writing:

Gripp H.Q

To the boy,

You fools, I said you'd be sorry! You wouldn't sell me your business, so I'm going to take it from you. I have kidnapped your parents, and if you ever want to see them again, you must do exactly what I say.

Leave the plans for all your inventions at the Spiny Cactus in the middle of the Flaming Desert. Once I have retrieved them I will free your parents. You have one week – and there'd better be no funny business!

Signed,
Ida Gripp,
Tycoon, Entrepreneur, Fat-cat

"Forget meeting at the Spiny Cactus," I thought to myself. "I need to rescue Mom and Pop."

I rushed outside to the large hut where I kept my Mechanimals. Ida had tried to force the lock, but had been unable to break in. I punched in the passcode and hurried to the shelf where I kept **Eagle-Eye**, my battery-powered kestrel.

I checked the battery was fully charged and then launched Eagle-Eye into the air. It climbed into the sky and set off across town towards a tall bamboo forest and the hills beyond. Now all I could do was wait and hope, and check that my Mechanimals were ready for action.

I oiled Steel-Skull's joints and filled his tank with hydrogen. My mechanical gorilla was formidable, but for all I knew Ida Gripp had an army of underlings on her side and I might need all the help I could get. I decided to take another Mechanimal as well. I chose my Armoured Armadillo – it's like a one-man tank, only better!

When Eagle-Eye came swooping back I checked the photos it had stored on its memory card. One showed some tall towers carved into

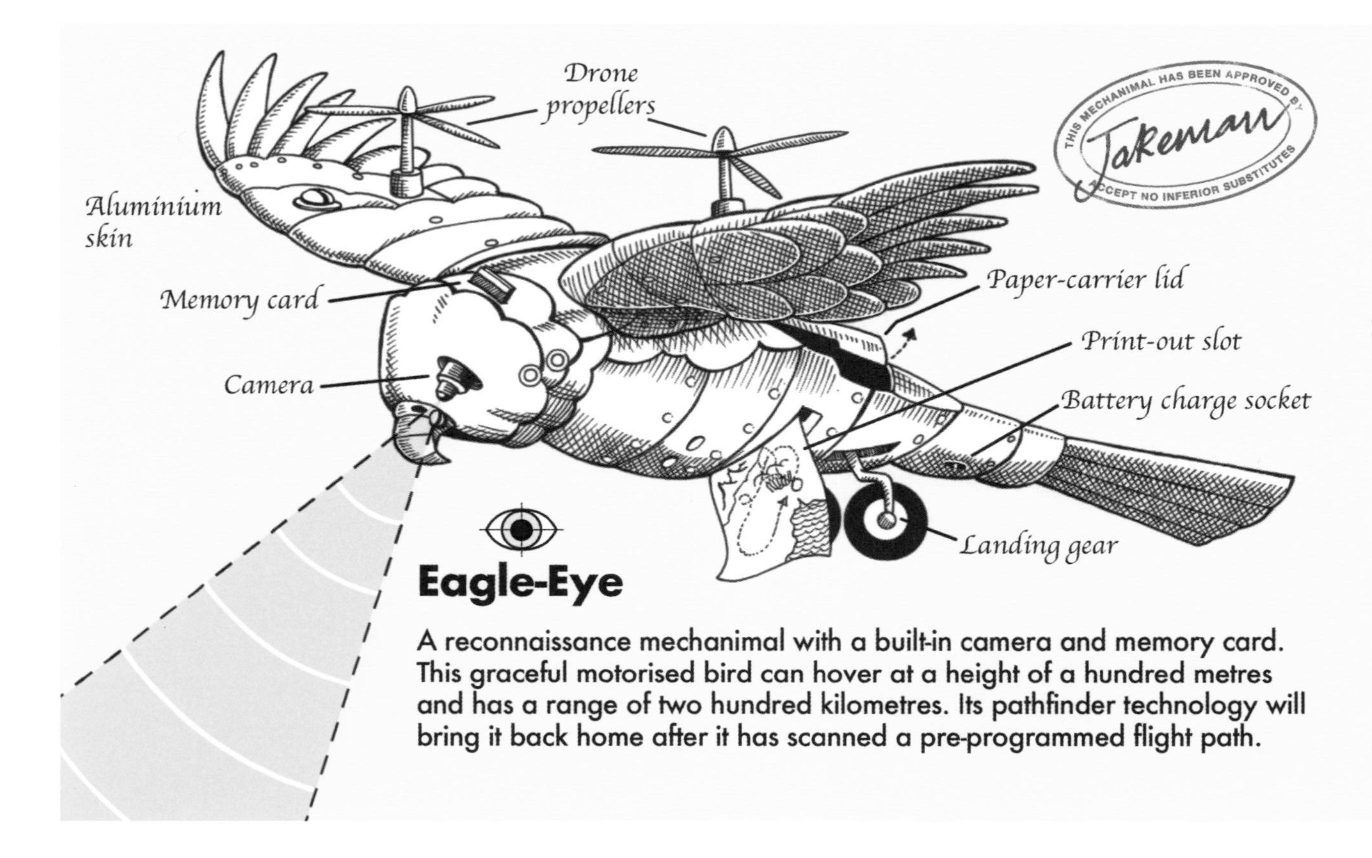

Eagle-Eye

A reconnaissance mechanimal with a built-in camera and memory card. This graceful motorised bird can hover at a height of a hundred metres and has a range of two hundred kilometres. Its pathfinder technology will bring it back home after it has scanned a pre-programmed flight path.

Jakeman's Mechanimal Spy Series Model No. 1 • Patent No. WJM 0364 the dark granite of a huge cliff. A flag fluttered at the top of a black pole, and on the flag was written: **Gripp Enterprises. Keep Out.**

I pressed a button on Eagle-Eye's tummy and it printed out a map. Gripp HQ was clearly marked. It was a long way off, on the side of a deep and desolate valley, but if I got a move on I should be able to make it in a few hours. Then I could take the despicable Ida Gripp by surprise.

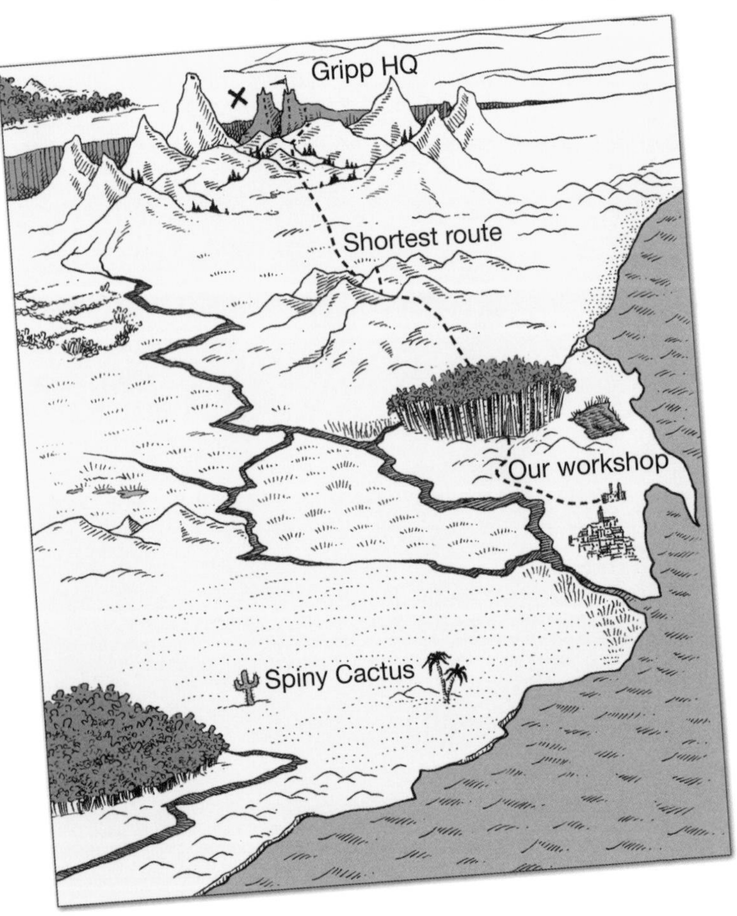

Mechanimals to the Rescue

It was the deep, dark dead of night when I steered the Armadillo along the High Street and out of town, its headlamp eyes illuminating the way ahead. Steel-Skull walked on all fours beside us, his joints squeaking, his big metal chest booming and his chimney emitting small puffs of water vapour.

We passed through the spooky forest of giant bamboo trees, their trunks rattling like dry bones, and then climbed into the freezing mists of Horrorscar Heights. Ice crystals formed in my hair and on my eyelashes as a cold wind swirled around me, howling like a lonesome and very hungry wolf.

STATS:

Top speed: 35 kph

Barging strength: 3000 kg/cm^2

Fire power: 30 rounds of gunge or 20 rounds of compressed air balls per minute

Steering handles and brakes

Steel shell

Gunge gun and compressed-air cannon

Armour-plated head

Flashing eyes

Defensive claws

Jakeman's Petal-Powered

Armoured Armadillo

A magnificent Mechanimal that can travel over any terrain, barge through most obstacles and is armed with a gunge gun that fires a quick-setting gel, turning any enemy it hits into a living statue!

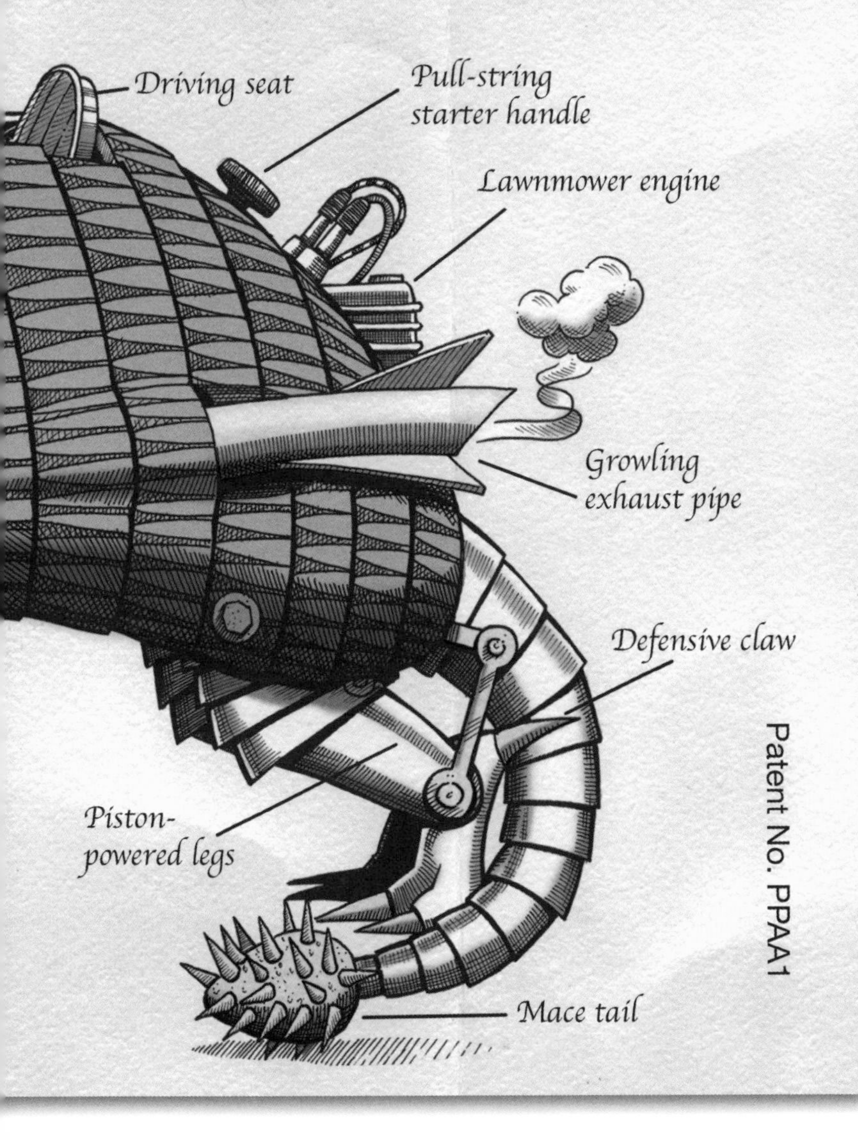

Patent No. PPAA1

By the time we'd descended the path on the other side, dawn was beginning to break and I was frozen solid. Steel-Skull cuddled me in his massive metal arms and the warmth from his whirring electric motor gradually warmed me up.

Feeling revived, I looked across the valley and let out a gasp. *Holy-moly!* There, silhouetted

against the early morning sky, were the towers of Gripp Enterprises. They looked like enormous chimneys and were pumping out plumes of choking smoke. Yuck. Whatever she was, Ida Gripp certainly wasn't concerned about polluting the atmosphere.

We trundled across the valley and onto a zig-zag path that climbed the side of the cliff. As we approached some tall, heavy doors set into the towers, one of the cretinous Cronies who had bullied me on my way to school leaped out from behind a pile of rocks. It was brandishing a wooden club.

"Who goes there?" he demanded in a bubbling, wheezing voice.

"I'm Will Jakeman. What's it got to do with you?" I said trying to sound bold and brave as a lot more Cronies began to appear, each one swinging a heavy club.

"We are Gripp Enterprises' security guards," the dribbling thing replied, eyeing my Mechanimals warily. "Now clear off or face the grisly consequences."

"We're not going anywhere until Ida Gripp frees my mom and pop," I said. "So what are you going to do about it?"

"This," he shouted, and the Cronies began flinging their short, heavy clubs high into the air. They whirled like propellers and bounced off my Armadillo's shell with reverberating clangs. Then the Cronies surged towards us.

"Watch out!" I cried.

Steel-Skull stood up, thumped his mighty chest and with a roar swept them aside with his massive arms. "GNNAAARGH!"

"Weeek, weeeeek!" the Cronies squealed as they went tumbling across the path.

"GNNAAARGH!" Steel-Skull bellowed again, and the petrified Cronies leaped straight over the cliff edge. They dropped into the deep gorge below and went bouncing away like rubber balls across the valley floor.

"Well done, Steel-Skull," I said, as I steered the Armadillo to face the tower doors. I switched its cannon from gunge-gun to compressed-air mode, and fired.

BOOF!

The doors were blown clean off their hinges and I drove the rumbling Armadillo inside. We entered a large, circular room at the base of one of the towers. A dozen doors were set all the way around, and on the far side a wide corridor stretched back into the cliff. Pipes sprouted from the walls like a tangle of tree roots and climbed up inside the tower to belch out thick, greasy smoke into the atmosphere high above. Ida Gripp was sitting at an enormous desk, calmly flicking away at an abacus and writing into a large ledger in front of her.

Inside Ida's Lair

"Well, well. Look who's here – I thought I told you to leave the plans at the Spiny Cactus," she said calmly, without bothering to look up. "I trust you have them with you?"

"Oh, well, actually – no," I said, starting to wish I had brought them with me.

"Then you must enjoy the dubious hospitality of my deep, dark dungeon until you change your mind, my dear," she said, and rang a small bell on her desk. When nothing happened she rang it again.

"Cronies, come here!" she bellowed.

"I think you'll find they've scarpered," I said. "Like rats from a sinking ship."

"Scarpered?" cried Ida, rising out of her chair with a thunderous look on her face. "Oh, the useless creatures."

Then she reached into her handbag, pulled out a strange pistol-shaped catapult and began to load it with what looked like a stripy hairpin from her beehive hairdo. Only it wasn't a stripy hairpin, but a weird wasp with a stinger as long as a pencil.

"This is going to sting like billy-o, you interfering little squirt," she snarled, and aimed the catapult straight at me.

"Quick, Steel-Skull!" I yelled, and my metal friend lunged forward and grabbed her wrist before she could fire. The catapult fell from her grasp and the wasp buzzed back up into her hair. Then Steel-Skull picked her up, flipped her upside down and held her dangling by the ankle.

"Put me down!" screeched Ida Gripp, beside herself with fury.

"Not until you've freed my mom and pop," I said.

"Give me your plans and we'll talk about it!" hissed Ida.

I gave a long sigh. "OK, Steel-Skull. You know what to do," I said.

"Ugh," he grunted, and carried her out of the tower door and held her over the edge of the precipice.

"Let them go," I demanded.

"Never," she snarled, but Steel-Skull loosened his hold, and she slipped a bit.

"Arrgh!" squealed Ida Gripp. "OK, I surrender! Let me go and I'll explain what's happened to your parents."

I nodded at Steel-Skull, and he put her back on the ground.

"What's going on?" I said, with an uneasy feeling. "Where are Mom and Pop?"

"Um, they escaped," said Ida Gripp, looking rather sheepish.

"I don't believe you," I said.

"It's true," said Ida Gripp. "Look, I'll show you. Come with me."

Steel-Skull and I followed her to a smelly dungeon in the tower's cellar, her heels clattering across the stone floor.

"See? I locked them in here, but they managed to get out."

"I still don't believe you," I said, peering around the empty cell. "If they escaped they would have gone straight home."

"I'm sure they would, but I sent my Cronies to track them down, and I'm afraid your mom and pop got sort of squished in the process," said Ida, with a sniggering sneer.

"Squished?" I cried, horrified. "What do you mean, squished?"

"Well, when my Cronies get over excited

they bounce around like manic rubber balls, and have a nasty habit of landing on things and, err… squishing them."

"Squishing!" I repeated in a strangled voice.

"Squishing, squashing, squidging," said Ida Gripp, with a shrug. "But never mind, they wouldn't have felt a thing."

I was shocked, and felt rooted to the spot. Then I pulled myself together, stormed out of the cell and quickly slammed the door, locking Ida inside.

"What are you doing? You can't leave me in here," she yelled.

"Well, if my poor old mom and pop can escape, it shouldn't be too much trouble for you, should it?" I said.

"Don't be hasty, boy. Let's discuss business. I would still luuurve to buy your inventions," cried Ida Gripp, as I climbed the cellar stairs. "Think what you could do with all that lovely money if you sold your plans to me."

"Come on, Steel-Skull," I said, ignoring her.

We left the tower and I climbed back into the Armadillo and started its motor. I felt stunned. Mom and Pop squished? I gunned the Armadillo's engine and drove home in shocked silence.

Everything was just as I'd left it, but it felt empty now. I tidied up Ida Gripp's mess as best I could and then collapsed on my bed and fell into a fitful sleep filled with nightmarish dreams.

What next, dear readers?

I couldn't believe it. Everything had changed and I was on my own once again. I missed my lovely mom and pop terribly, but if there was one thing they had taught me, it was how to fend for myself. I was determined to become the best inventor I could possibly be and hope they would have been proud of me.

Home Alone

So, at the ripe old age of twelve I had inherited my very own inventing workshop. To help me get over the terrible loss of Mom and Pop, I threw myself into my work, staying up late into the night and inventing all sorts of wonderful Mechanimals.

I invented other things too: the Self-making Bed; Jakeman's Athletic Trousers that make your legs run super-fast, and Will's Wonderful Suction Shoes that enable you to climb up walls. Opposite are some sketches I did of them.

Inventing is such fun, everyone should give it a go.

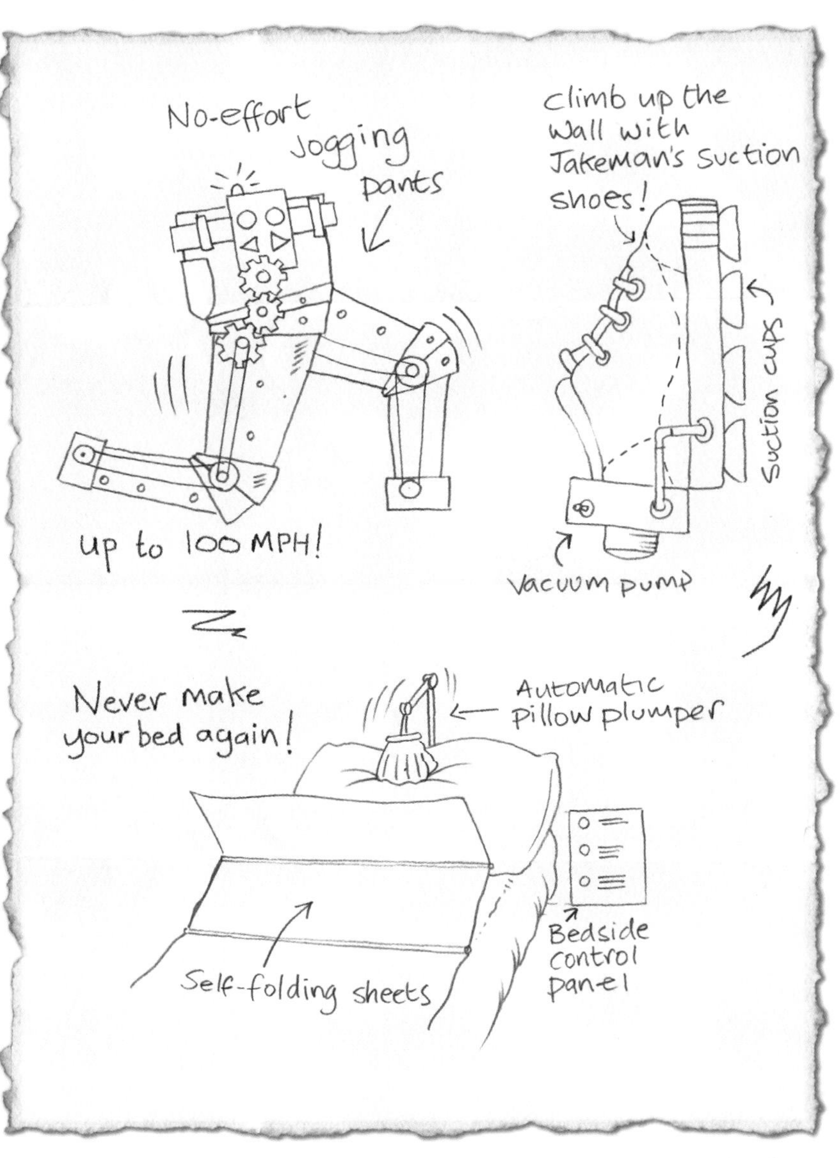

In fact why not use the blank pages overleaf to draw some of *your* brilliant ideas. Go on, let your imagination run wild:

Inventor's name: ....

My invention is called: ....

....

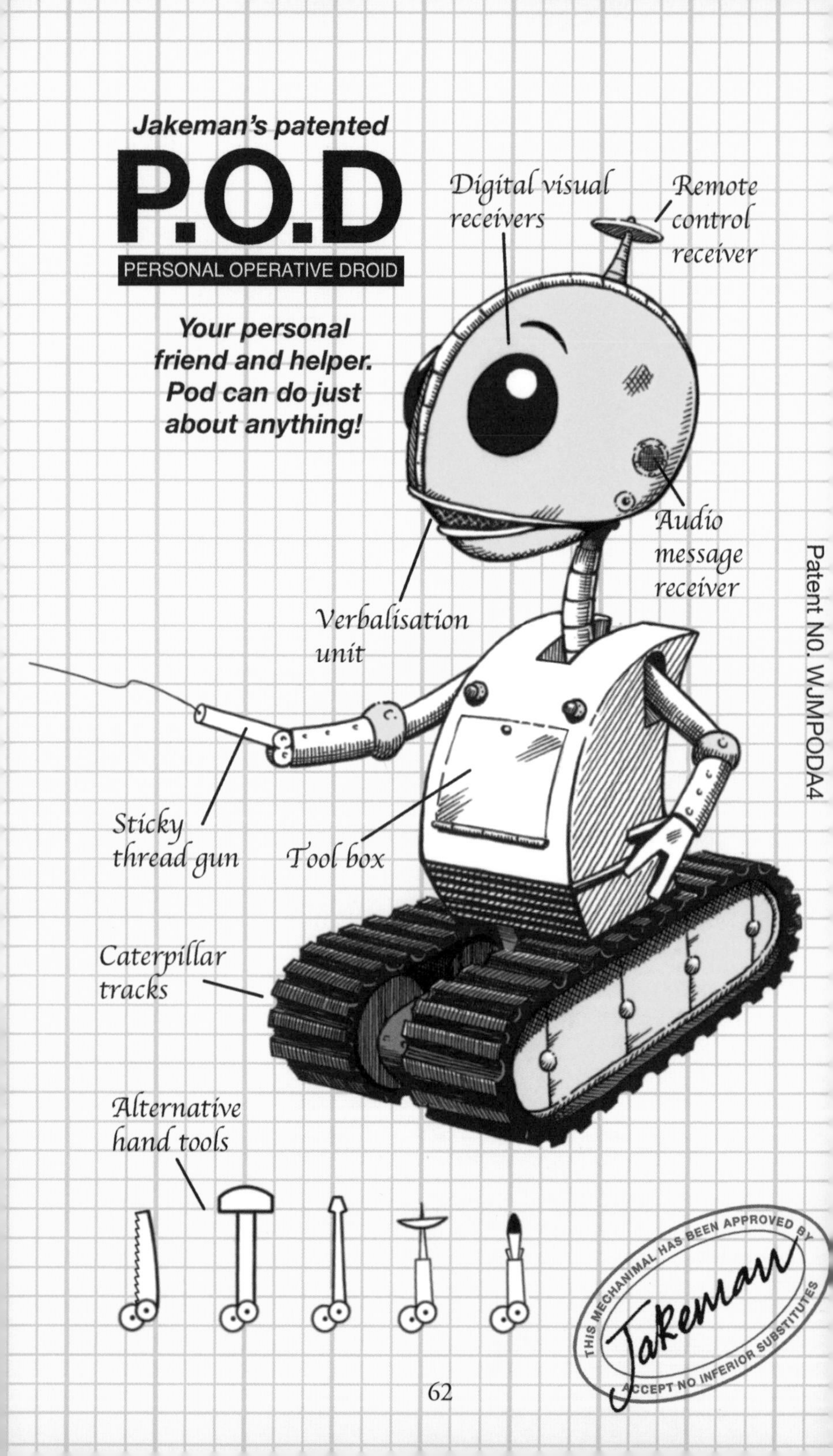
Jakeman's patented
P.O.D
PERSONAL OPERATIVE DROID
Your personal friend and helper. Pod can do just about anything!
Digital visual receivers
Remote control receiver
Audio message receiver
Verbalisation unit
Sticky thread gun
Tool box
Caterpillar tracks
Alternative hand tools
Patent N0. WJMPODA4
THIS MECHANIMAL HAS BEEN APPROVED BY
Jakeman
ACCEPT NO INFERIOR SUBSTITUTES

Soon my Mechanimals became so popular I had to invent robots to help me build them all. I called them P.O.Ds, Personal Operative Droids, and they were funny and friendly and had a variety of attachments for doing different jobs. With their help my dilapidated workshop gradually grew into a large factory. In memory of Mom, I made sure it was completely carbon-neutral to help protect Urf's environment.

Years came and went, and the P.O.Ds and Mechanimals became my brand new family. I could talk to them about my problems and my dreams, and they would reply with various grunts and whistles and clangs.

I understood them all perfectly, and we would often stay up late communicating about science and inventing and the downright nastiness of Ida Gripp. I'm sure their computer brains were starting to take on a life of their own. I learned a lot from my Mechanimals, especially Steel-Skull who was quite the philosopher!

When I had built enough Mechanimals to fill a storeroom, I put an advert in our local paper, *The Urf Today*.

Going on an Adventure?

Being Terrorised by a Rampaging Raptor?

Then get yourself down to

Jakeman's Factory of Inventions!

15 Invention Place, Cockle Bay, Urf

And buy your very own

Marvellous Mechanimal

Come and choose from our vast range
Prices from 10 gronags to 15,000 gronags

Satisfaction Guaranteed!

It wasn't long before people were knocking on my door. Scientists, explorers and anyone scared of being eaten by a dangerous predator, all wanted a Mechanimal of their own.

I would escort them around my warehouse, past flying Mechanimals and burrowing Mechanimals, and into the wonderful Mega-Mechanimal department. There was something for nearly everyone!

One of my first customers was world famous wildlife expert Amelia Bloop, who needed a machine to take her across the boggy mudflats of The Ravern, a remote and steamy jungle river.

The Ravern is alive with nasty creatures, and Amelia needed something that was light on its feet and could protect her against ferocious foes. I hadn't got anything suitable for the job, so I put my thinking cap on and came up with just the thing. It was light and fast and heavily armed, even if it was a little bird-brained – the **Sensational Clockwork Swamp Hopper!**

After some simple operating instructions, and a quick test-run around the factory yard, Amelia was ready to set off.

Will Jakeman's Sensational
Clockwork Swamp Hopper

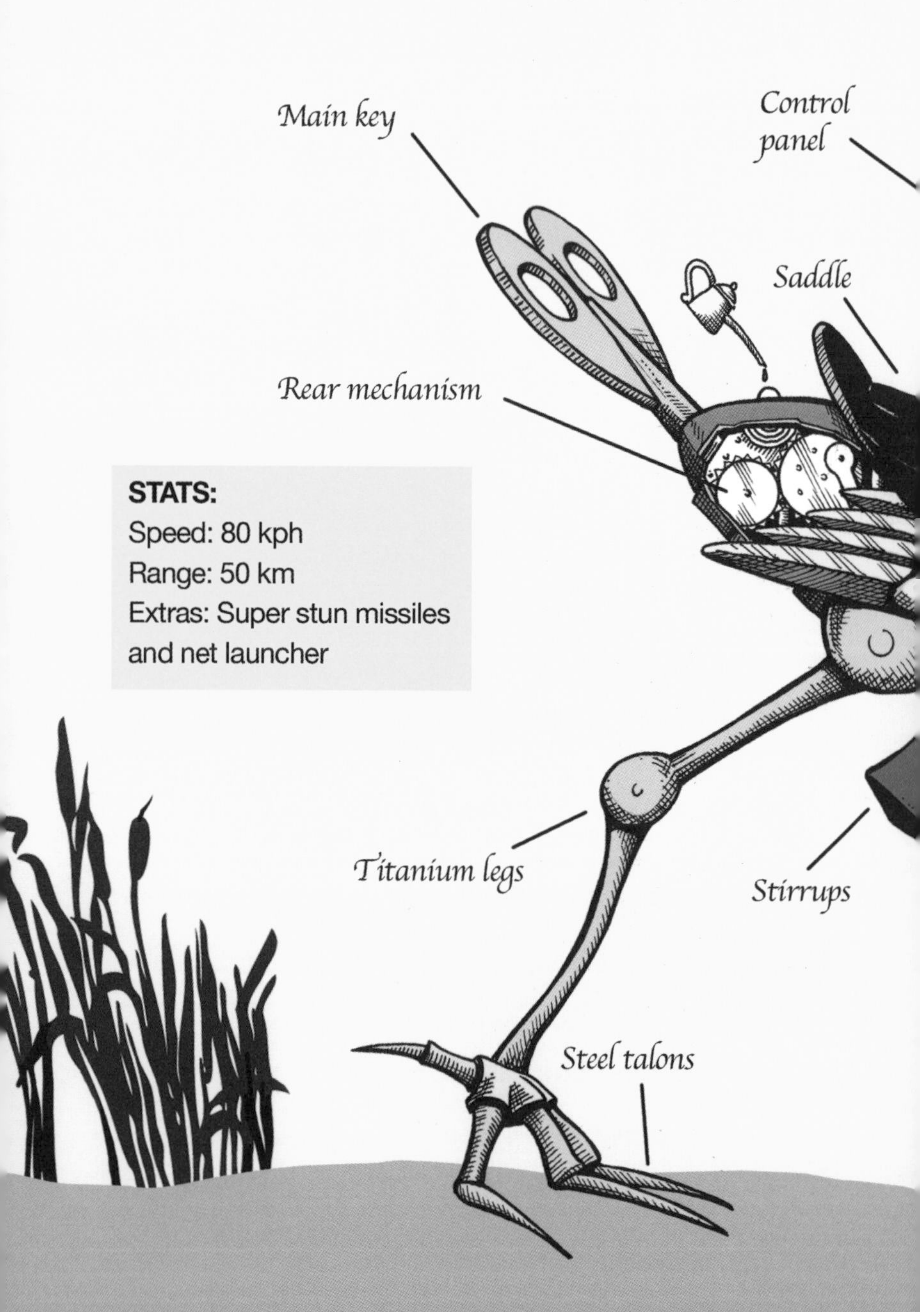

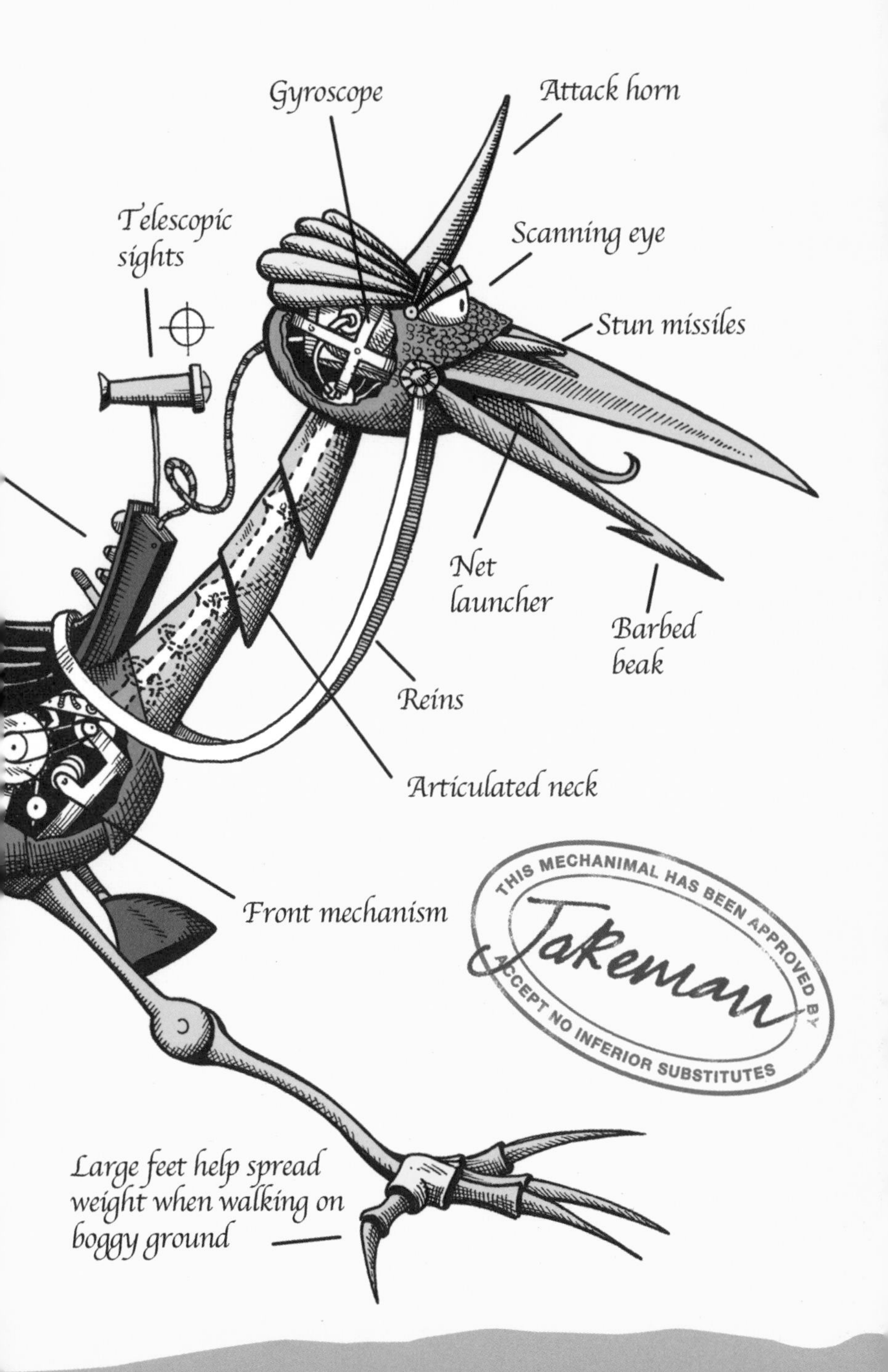

Patent No. WJM0428

Amelia's Adventure

Swampy the Swamp Hopper was perfect for Miss Bloop's expedition. His light frame and large feet allow him to walk across the boggiest ground, and his clockwork motor would carry Amelia for fifty kilometres before it needed rewinding. Swampy proved to be a real hero too, and saved Amelia's skin more than once.

Just take a look at what our local newspaper had to say…

URF NEWS

TERROR IN THE SWAMP!

Amelia Bloop, the renowned naturalist, rock climber, gourmet cook, blogger and influencer, told our reporter how she nearly came to a sticky end on her latest daredevil adventure.

As Amelia crossed the wide, boggy estuary of the River Ravern on the back of Swampy the Swamp Hopper, a huge Snapping Eel rose out of the mud and launched a savage attack.

Swampy struck back, grabbing the fearsome creature in its bill, then tossing it high into the air and swallowing it in one gulp!

Before our intrepid hero could catch her breath, a swarm of flying Coptor Fish flew out from a clump of reeds and made straight for her, spitting a hail of deadly darts.

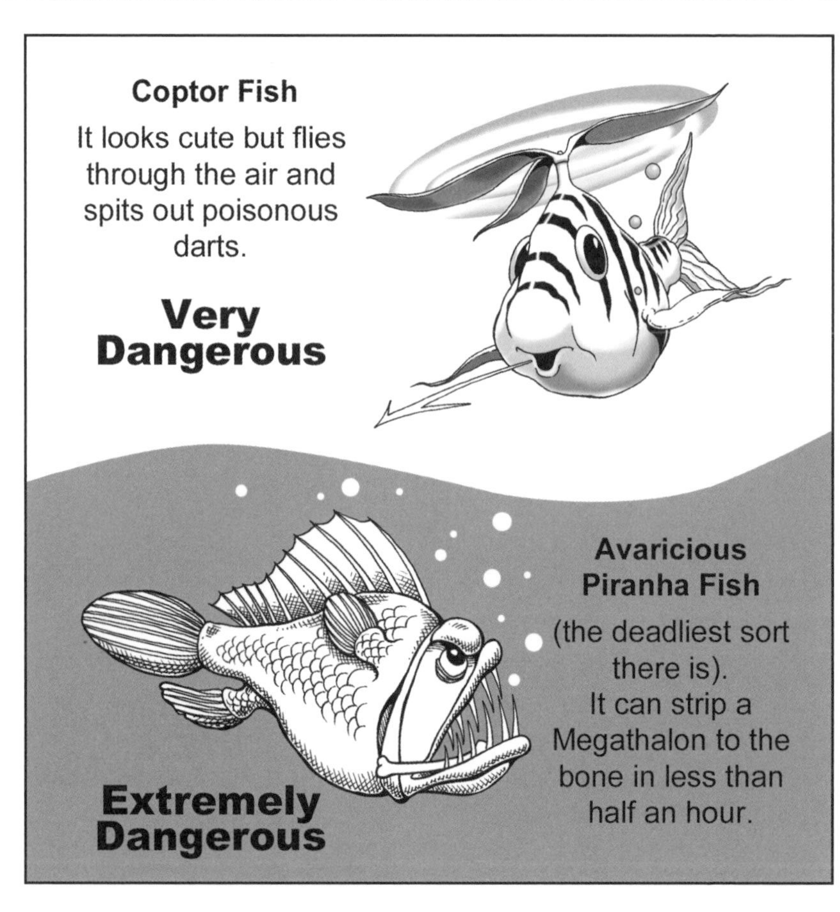

"It was terrifying," said Miss Bloop. "But I quickly fired some of Swampy's stun missiles, and the shoal of dazed Coptor Fish dropped into the river below."

The steaming waters began to churn as the Coptor Fish were set upon by a pack of deadly piranha. The piranha even leaped out of the river and tried to snap at Miss Bloop's ankles, but Swampy speedily carried her to safety on his long metal legs.

It was then Amelia spied the creature that has since made her famous. Grazing on the riverbank was a most remarkable animal – an animal hitherto unknown to science. It had the jaws of a crocodile and the blubbery body of a hippopotamus, and she immediately named it the Crocapotamus!

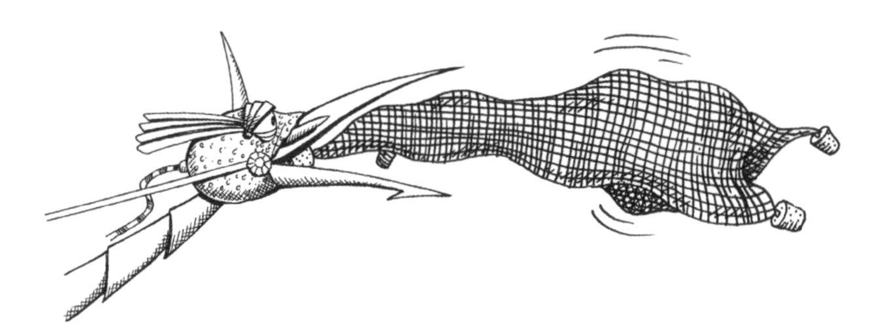

"I wanted to study the creature more closely, but I was worried it might attack me," Amelia told our reporter. "So I fired a net from Swampy's beak to trap it.

"The huge animal began to bellow and wriggle, trying to escape – but I edged forward, speaking to it softly to try and calm it down. As it turned out, I was worried about nothing. The Crocapotamus was as tame as a puppy dog, and so very lonely it followed me all the way home."

The Crocapotamus now lives a peaceful life in Amelia's back garden, and the two of them have become world famous celebrities!

"I couldn't have done it without dear old Swampy, though," said Amelia. "He's simply the best. Everyone should have a Will Jakeman Mechanimal of their own!"

A Menagerie of Mechanimals

Amelia's amazing story filled the newspapers and had all sorts of people clamouring to own one of my Mechanimals.

First came Darna, the leader of a remote jungle village. Her people were being terrorized by a horrific Night Demon that filled their dreams and turned them into quivering wrecks. To tackle this haunting apparition she chose my **Solar-powered Tiger**, a magnificent Mechanimal powered by a solar panel on its

Darna, the village leader

back. It was sleek and swift and fearsome, and its bite was so powerful it could crack a boulder in half.

Night after lonely night the mechanical tiger prowled through the jungle, watching and waiting. When the Demon finally appeared the tiger pounced, its eyes flashing red and its roar shaking the leaves on the trees.

"*RAAAAR!*"

"*EEEEK!*" The petrified Night Demon let out a bloodcurdling scream, opening its mouth so wide it swallowed itself by mistake and was never seen again!

The villagers were overjoyed, and swore an oath of loyalty, promising to come to my aid if I ever found myself in trouble.

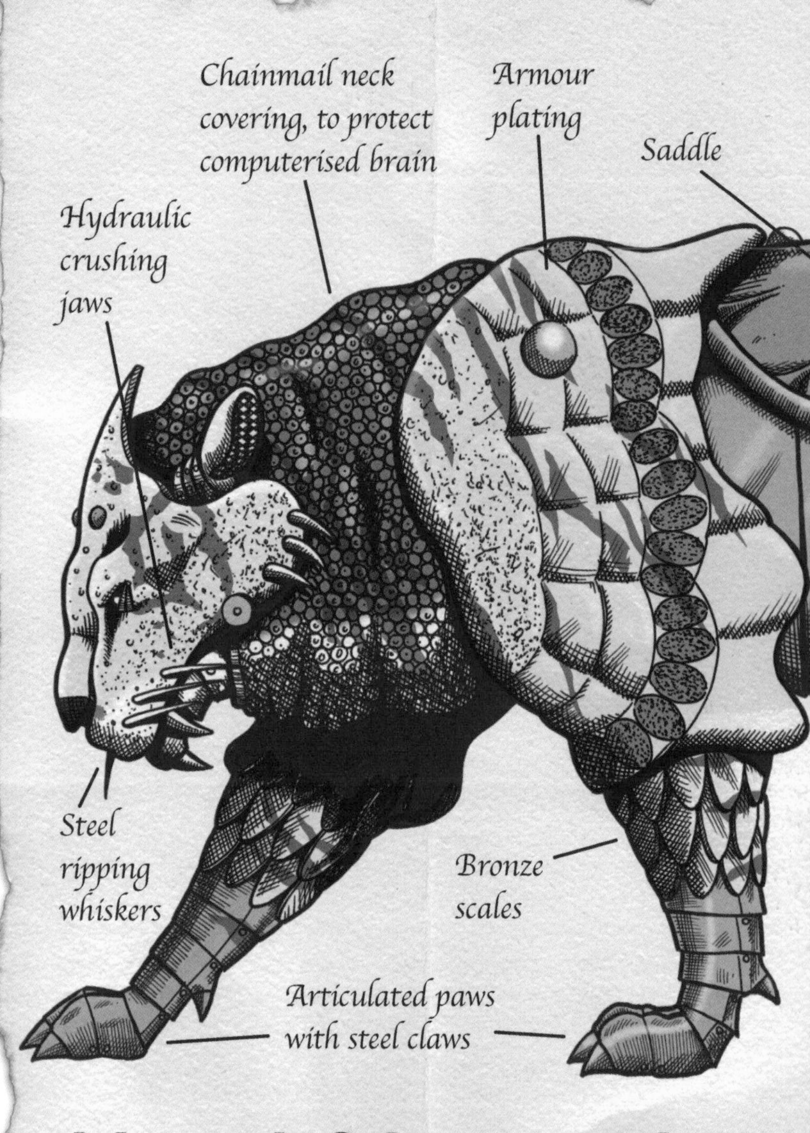

Jakeman's Solar-powered, Computerised Tiger with Hydraulic Crushing Jaws

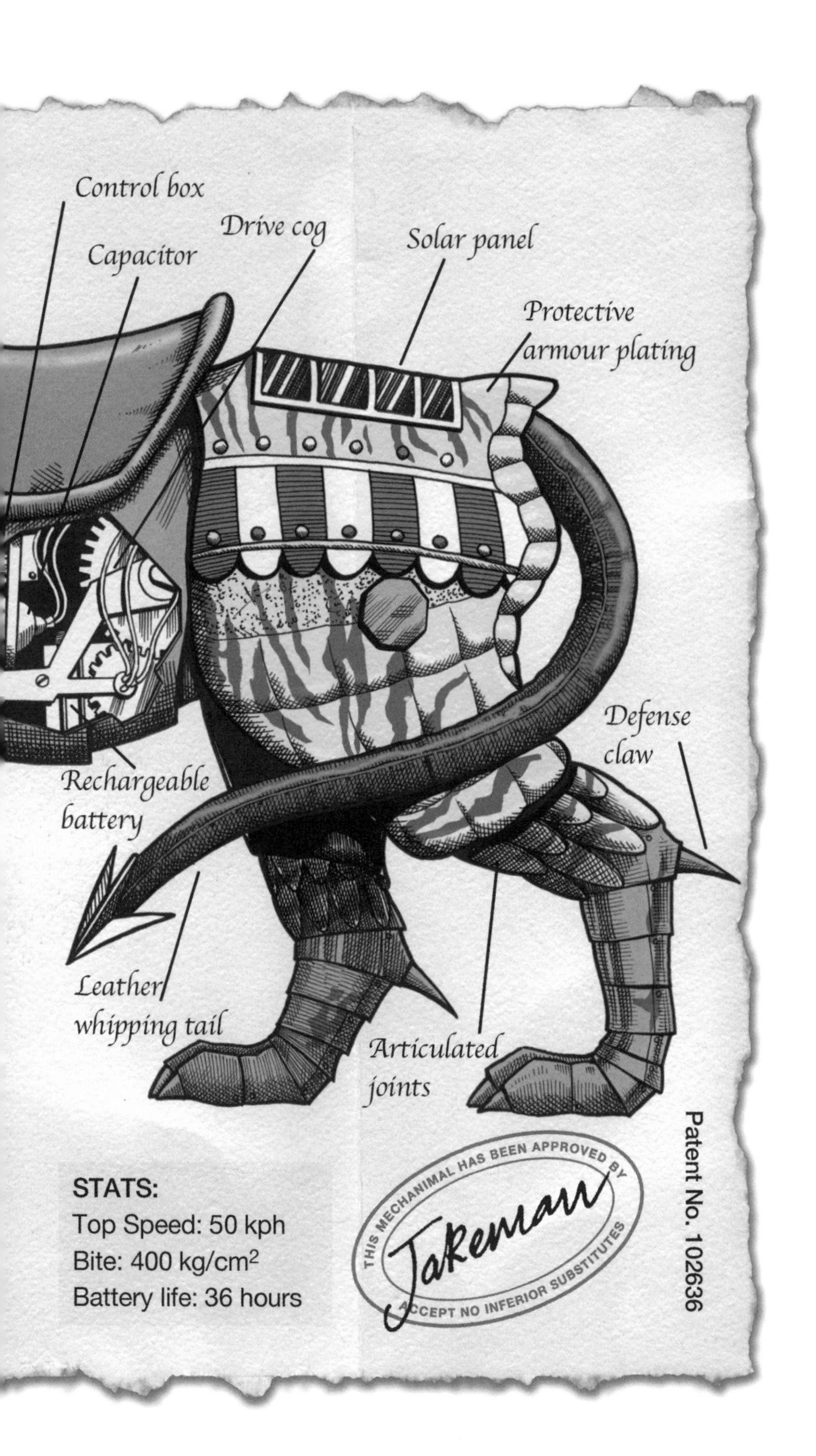

STATS:
Top Speed: 50 kph
Bite: 400 kg/cm^2
Battery life: 36 hours

One of my all-time favourite Mechanimals was Stompo, the **Hydrogen-powered battling Bulldozer Elephant**. I gave him to the King of Bhamia, who was in a terrible fix – a horrible potentate had invaded his country, leading an army of ferocious chimps and a battalion of war elephants.

Dear old Stompo led the counter-attack, ridden by Princess Maya, the King's brave daughter. A terrible battle ensued – arrows and spears flew through the air and the potentate's trumpeting elephants charged. Stompo's metal

sides were bashed and dented, but his swivelling cannons fired round after round of ten-pin bowling balls. The chimps were scattered like skittles, and the terrified potentate and his war elephants were driven from the land in disarray.

Stompo was awarded a medal for bravery beyond the call of duty, and the King sent me a message proclaiming me an absolute genius, and that Bhamia would be forever in my debt!

WILL JAKEMAN'S

HYDROGEN-POWERED BATTLING BULLDOZER ELEPHANT

Stompo is someone you would definitely want on your side in an argument. He can charge at 30 kph and demolish a whole building in seconds.

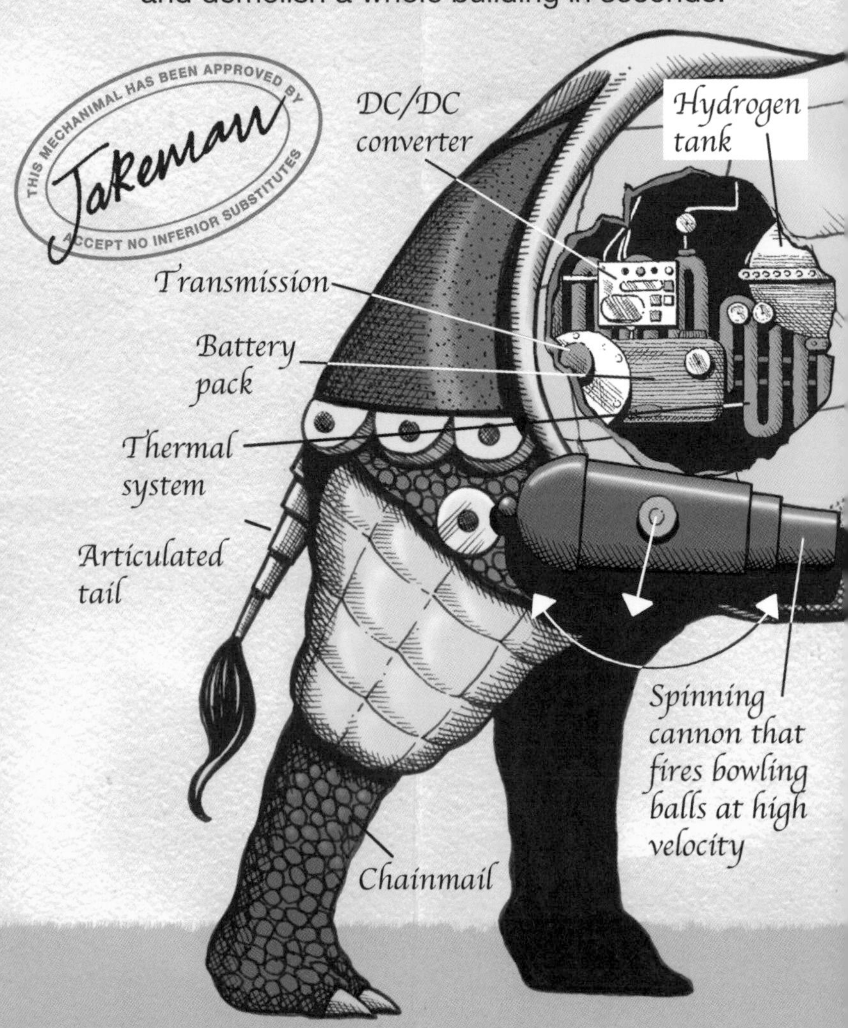

STATS:

0 to 30 kph: 20 seconds

Stomping power: 5000 kg/cm^2

Fire power: Ten bowling balls per minute

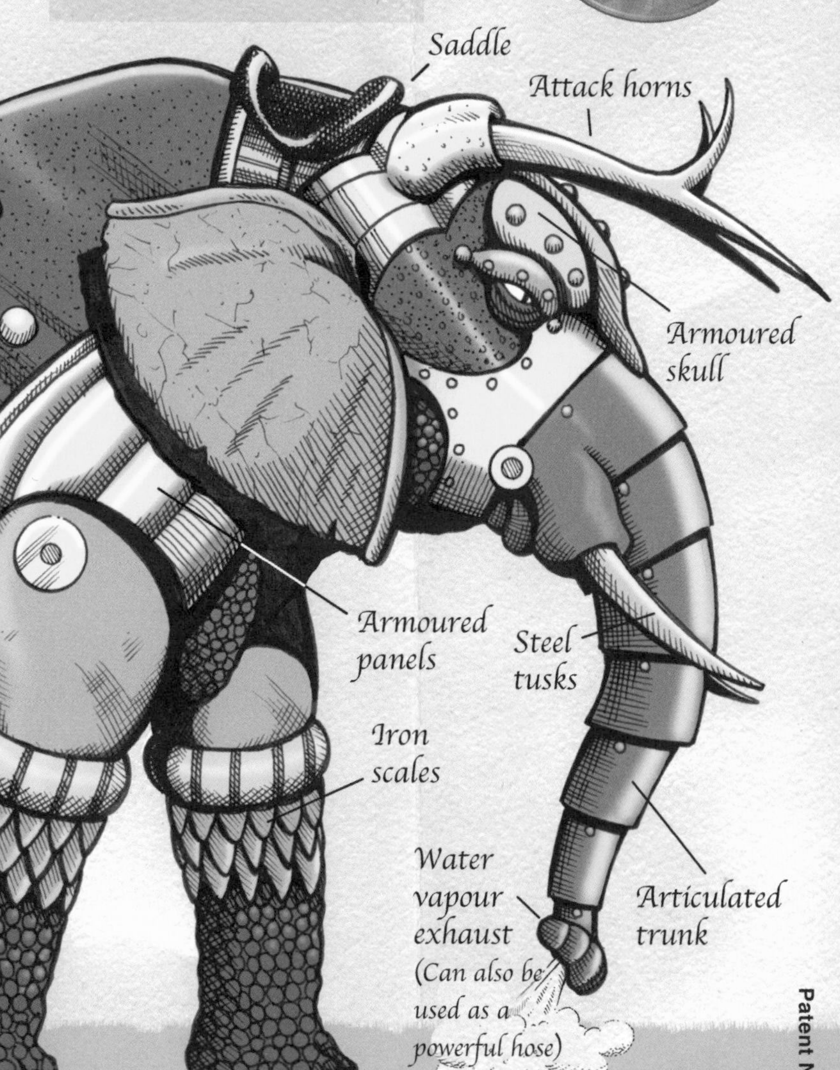

Patent No. 102634

Fearless Freddie

Fearless Freddie

I was always working on new ideas, and it wasn't long before I received an order from Fearless Freddie Fortescue-Scott. Yes, *that* Fearless Freddie – the world famous underwater explorer.

He was getting ready for a new and perilous mission – to hunt down the mythical Vipersquid, a terrible monster that lives in the blackest depths of Lunar Lake. Freddie asked me to design him an underwater Mechanimal to take on his quest. So I did – two Mechanimals in one!

The **Chemical-powered Crustacean Hover-sub** and the **Powder-propelled Jet Swordfish**.

The Swordfish was kept in the Hover-sub's storage hold for emergencies. To ride it you had to straddle its body, put your feet in the stirrups and steer with the handlebars behind its head.

The right handle was also the throttle – when you twisted it, a valve opened and water dripped onto a special powder, creating lots of gas. The gas would rush down an exhaust pipe into the sea, driving the swordfish forward. It was super quick and could leap like a dolphin.

The Crustacean Hover-sub looked like a huge, prehistoric crab and could go much deeper than the Swordfish. It was a hovercraft, a speedboat and a submarine all rolled into one! It had powerful spotlights for working in the blackest ocean depths and two massive claws to carry out remote-controlled, underwater experiments. It was an absolute corker!

When it was in boat mode a harmless gas powered a turbine that span the propeller, while in flight mode the gas was diverted to hover pads and the heavy Mechanimal rose into the air.

◆

Jakeman's

Chemical-powered Crustacean Hover-sub

STATS: Max speed: 40 knots at sea;
30 knots submerged; 50 kph in hover mode
Max dive depth: 1,000 metres
2 chemo tabs per 1,000 nautical miles
Claws: 150 tons of crushing force

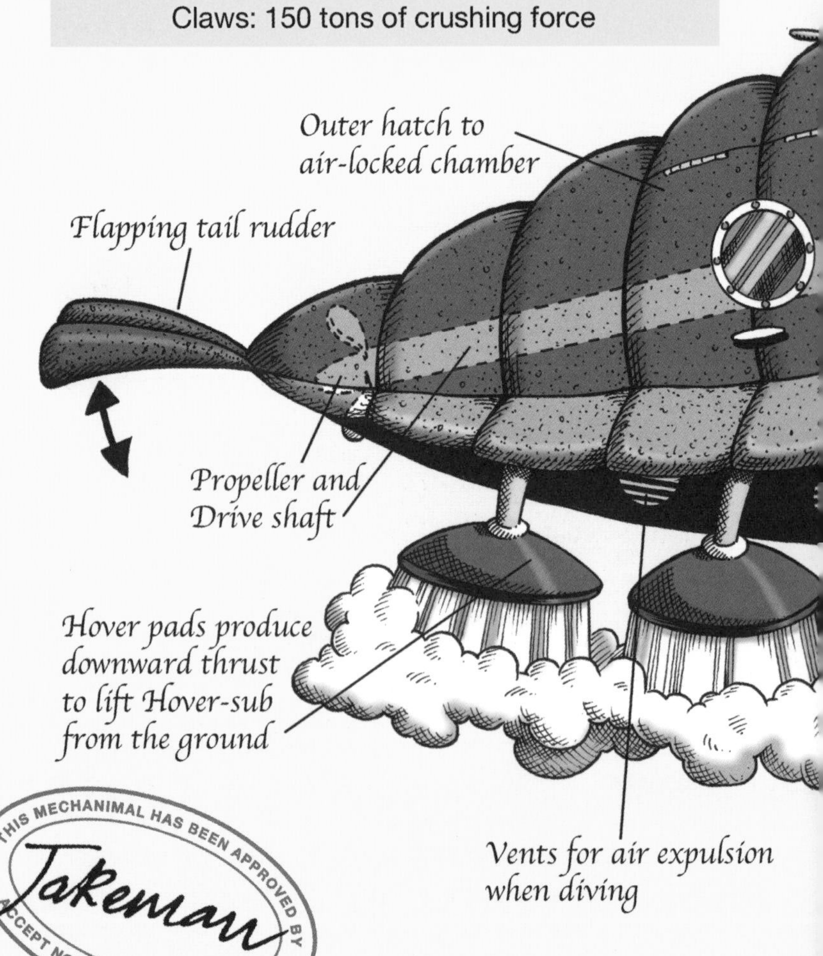

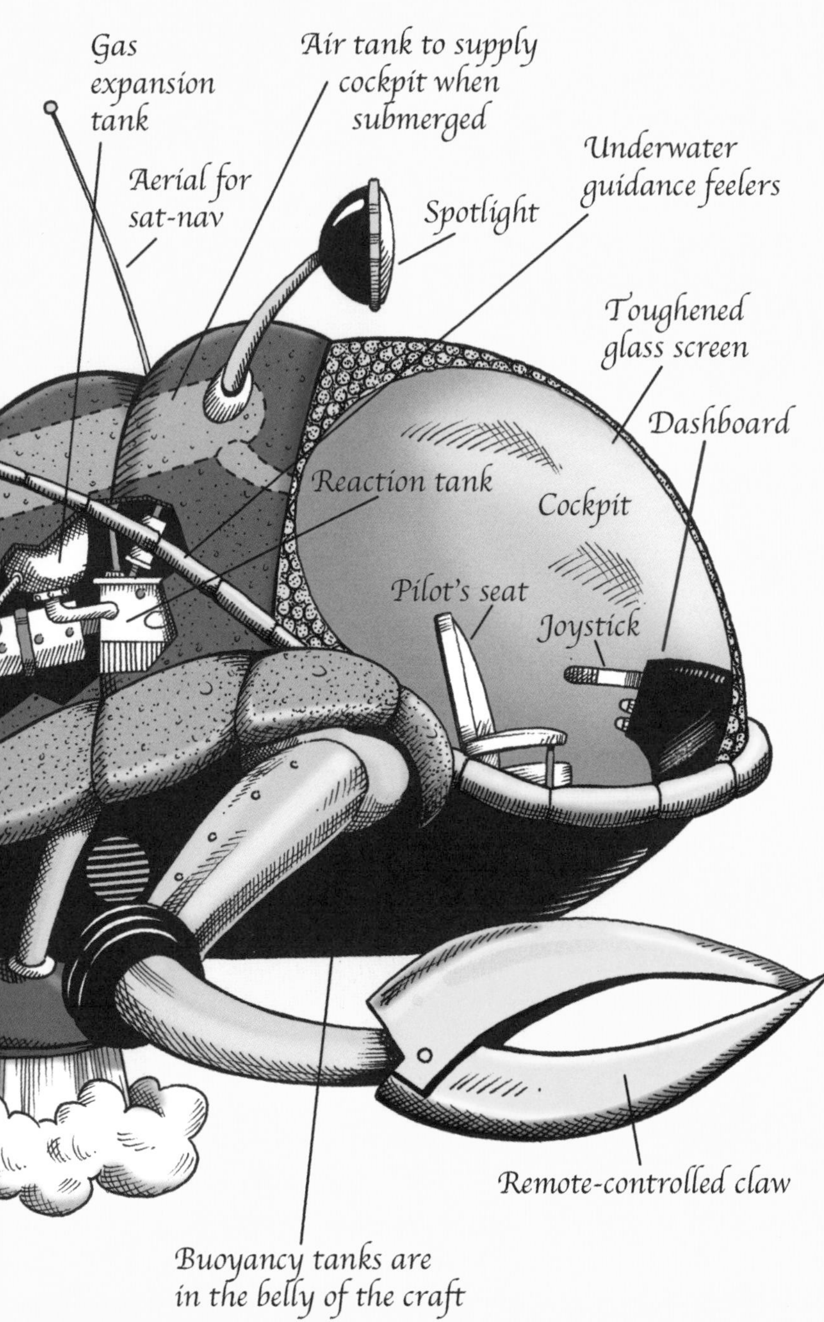

Patent No. 204936

Freddie was absolutely thrilled with both my inventions, and Urf TV made a programme about his dangerous adventure called…

PANIC AT LUNAR LAKE!

Good evening, ladies and gentlemen. Freddie Fortescue-Scott needs no introduction. He's dived to the bottom of the Midnight Sea, fought sharks single-handedly and cleaned the teeth of a monstrous killer whale.

We join him as he sets off in a Jakeman Hover-sub to track down the Vipersquid, a leviathan that crushes whole cruise ships in its writhing tentacles.

Freddie climbed aboard the Hover-sub, rose high above Jakeman's Factory and set off at full speed. He was soon flying through the perilous peaks of the Jagged Mountains.

He travelled for hour after lonely hour. Then, suddenly, he saw the black waters of Lunar Lake below him.

Freddie put the Hover-sub into a nose-dive. Its engines roared and rattled as he splashed into the forbidding lake.

Down he went, down to the deepest depths. The Hover-sub's headlights cut through the black water, but Freddie couldn't see any sign of the vile Vipersquid. And then, oh my goodness...

AARRRGH! IT'S HORRIBLE!

The Vipersquid grabbed the Hover-sub, squeezing it in its mighty coils until it began to crumple. Freddie ran to the hold, climbed onto the Powder-propelled Swordfish and zoomed out through the sub's escape hatch.

He raced for the surface, weaving between the Vipersquid's deadly coils. Would he make it?

JAKEMAN'S POWDER-PROPELLED JET SWORDFISH

A Sea-going Mechanimal

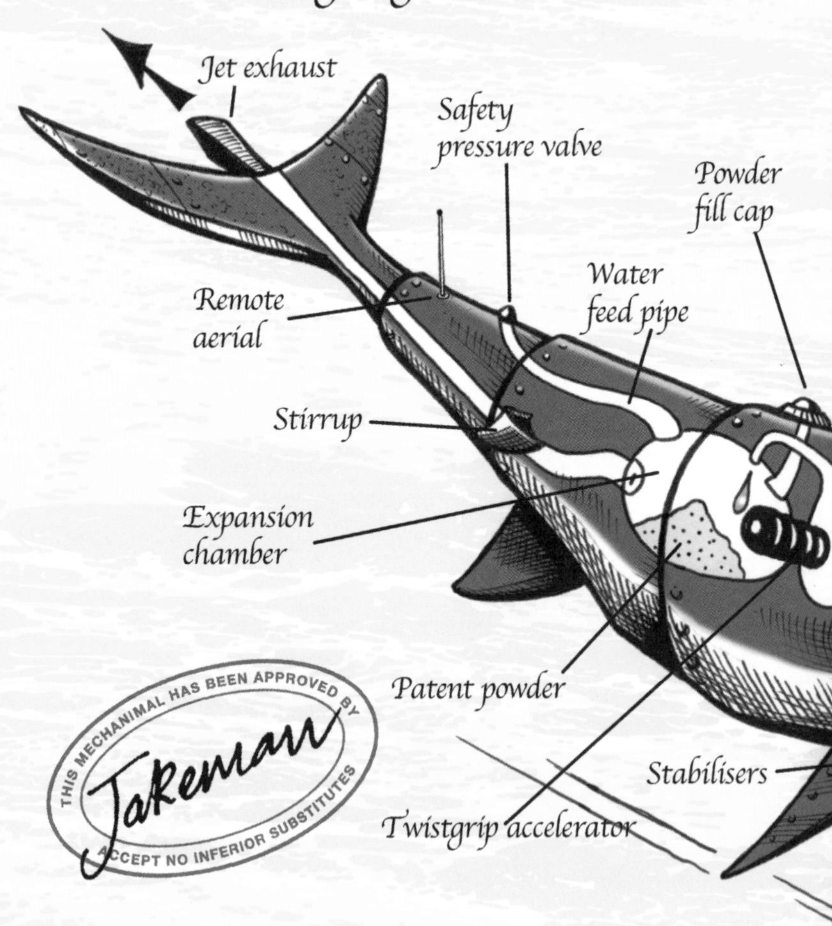

Patent No. 113236

STATS:
Max speed: 50 knots
320 brake fishpower
0–50 in 3 seconds

Chemical formula for Jakeman's gas producing powder:
NaHCO3+R2UST3+H20 = FzzzzPop!

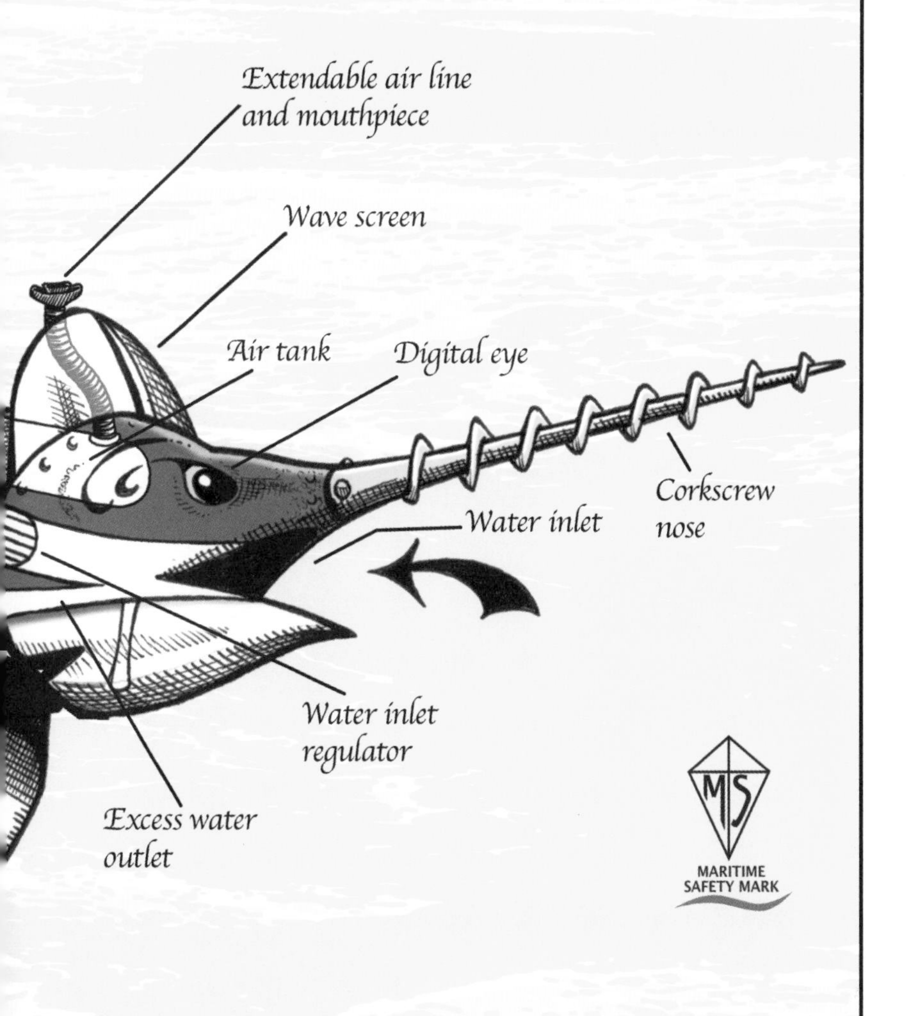

Freddie leaped from the lake, chased by the Vipersquid's hissing tentacles...

...then raced for the shore as the squid surfaced in an explosion of foam and ploughed through the water after him.

Freddie just managed to make it to the shore as a viper grabbed the Swordfish and crushed it in its jaws.

In a petrified panic Freddie activated the S.O.S button on his Jakeman tracking device, and then collapsed in a quivering heap of fear!
S.O.S!

Back at his factory, the ingenious inventor Will Jakeman received Freddie's call for help and raced to his Mechanimal warehouse. He leaped aboard his Hydraulic Bison and raced off at top speed.

Jakeman found the explorer still shivering with fear. He didn't utter a word the whole journey home, but just stared straight ahead with wide, petrified eyes. The Vipersquid had scared him witless.

*And that, dear viewers, was the end of Freddie's adventures. He was too nervous to ever go exploring again, but kindly Will Jakeman offered him a job at his wonderful factory, helping him make more marvellous, motorised Mechanimals!**

*Check out the **Hydroelectric Attack Shark** at the end of this book. Fearless Freddie helped design it, and it's a corker!

Jakeman's Patented Hydraulic Bison

Liquid pressure chamber & pump
Hydraulic piston
Reservoir
Excess gas release valve
Thick leather hide, stitched and riveted
Main flywheel
Fast fuel fermentation tank

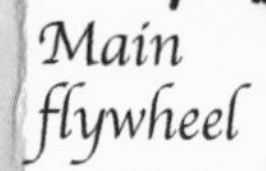

STATS:

Energy: Hydraulic power

Fuel: Fermented grass that produces gas. This gas is piped into a liquid filled chamber, subjecting it to enormous pressure. The liquid then pushes the pistons that work the cogs that drive the bison forward.

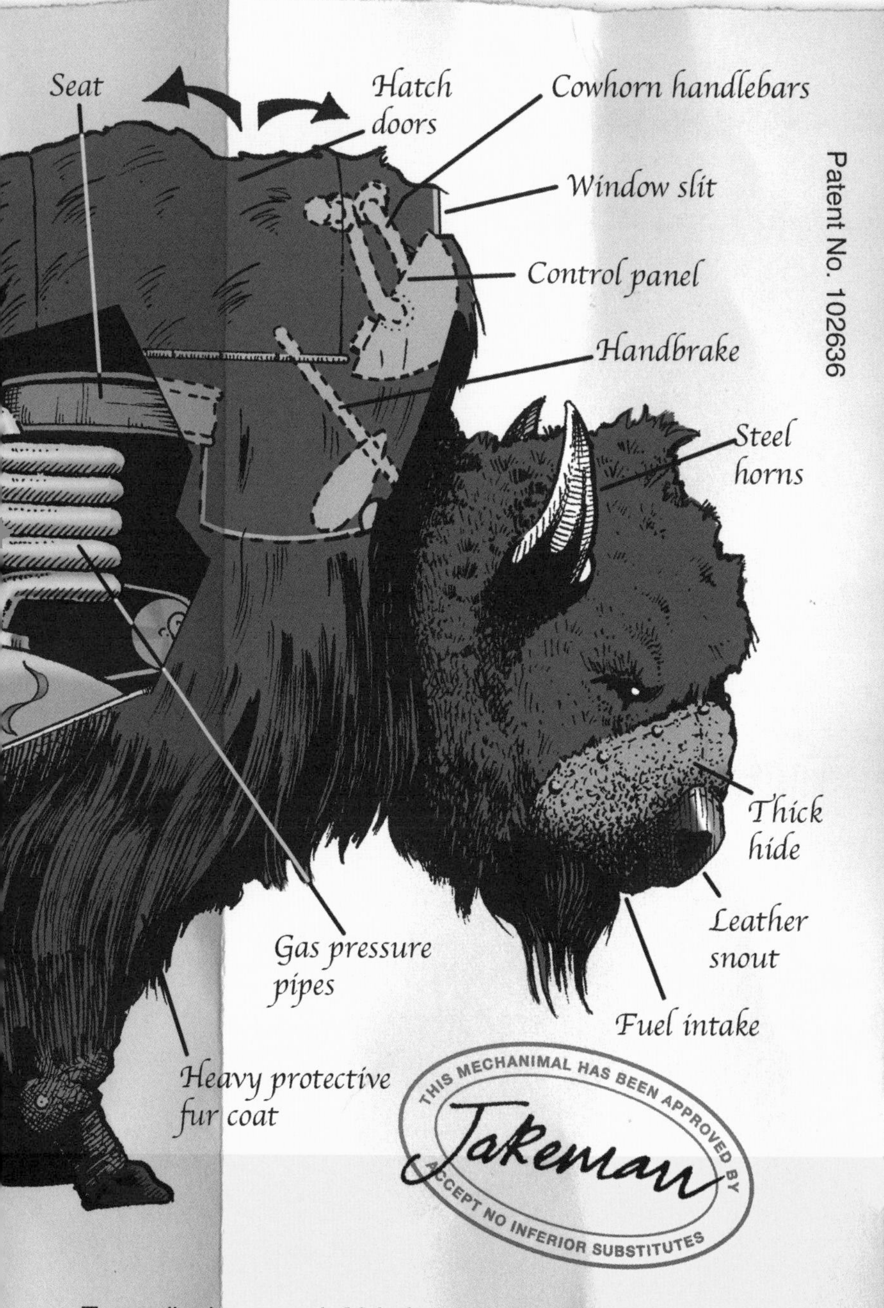

Patent No. 102636

Top galloping speed: 80 kph
Stopping distance: 200 metres at 60 kph
Barging power: 3,500 kg/cm^2
Scare factor: 9.5

You won't believe it, readers!

A Selfie, aged 40!

After all these amazing adventures I didn't think things could get any more exciting. Then, squash me flat with a steamroller, many years later and just when I was least expecting it, my world went absolutely bonkers.

Again!

The Return of Ida Gripp!

Ever since Ida Gripp had kidnapped Mom and Pop, I'd increased security and placed early warning monitors all over the surrounding countryside. Small crab-like Mechanimals the size of biscuits scuttled about, projecting thin laser

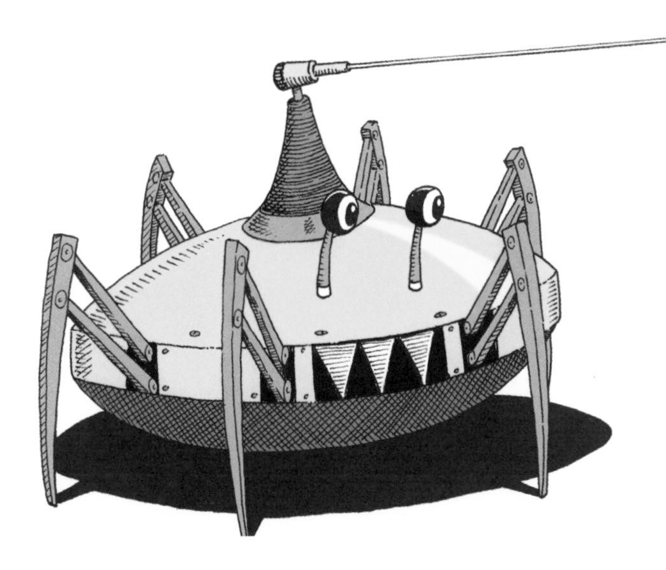

beams of light. When something broke one of the beams, an alarm went off in my workshop.

So, when the alarm began to buzz one morning, and carried on buzzing like a demented bee, I deployed my Eagle-Eye kestrel to see what all the fuss was about. I'd fitted it with a video camera that sent live images back to my workshop computer, and I watched intently as the kestrel flew towards the problem.

Holy-moly! Imagine my shock when I saw Ida Gripp leading an army of Cronies out of the

Bamboo Forest and heading in my direction. And not only Cronies but packs of Horror Hounds, too. For a moment I wasn't sure what to do. Then I had an idea. There was only one thing for it – I would have to muster an army of all my Mechanimals and meet Ida's hordes on open ground, before they reached our factory.

I raced to the warehouse and started up my Mechanimals, flicking switches to put them into autopilot mode.

"Listen up, Mechanimals!" I announced. "Ida Gripp is on her way with a vast and ruthless army. If we don't stop them we'll be under Ida's merciless rule forever more. Are you up for the fight?"

"Psst, bzzz, vrrrum," replied my wonderful metal friends.

I knew I could rely on them but I was worried that we would be outnumbered so I released a flock of tiny mechanical sparrows that tweeted "S.O.S" in Morse code. They flew off in every direction and

I hoped someone, somewhere would answer their call.

Then I climbed into the driving seat of my very latest Mechanimal, Will Jakeman's **Scuttling Scorpion.** *(See my diagram near the back of this book).* Driven by clockwork it could scurry happily along at 40 kph. The stings on its tail squirted a potent itching powder that would bring a T. Rex up in hives, and its snapping claws could peel open the top of a car in seconds.

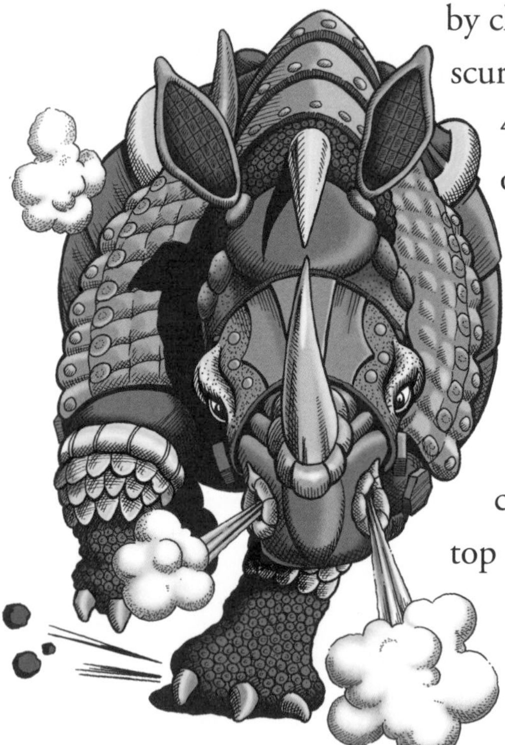

I drove the scorpion out of the warehouse followed by Ronald, my **Steam-powered Rhino**. I love Ronald – he's as powerful as a steamroller and as faithful as a dog, but I don't use him much as he isn't totally eco-friendly!

After Ronald came the Hydraulic Bison, and then good old Fearless Freddie riding Swampy the Swamp Hopper mark 2. They were followed by the Armoured Armadillo, then Steel-Skull of course, and twenty slithering, fire-spitting snakes.

I also marshalled a battalion of P.O.Ds, my Personal Operative Droids, and last but not least, **Mad Dog** – my latest canine pet.

We marched down the street, watched by a crowd of astonished townsfolk. Then out across the heath and off towards the Bamboo Forest we went, an army of clanking Mechanimals!

As we reached the brow of a low hill, we saw Ida Gripp's army appear on the opposite ridge. I had been right, there were thousands of them. We were hopelessly outnumbered, and my blood ran cold with fear.

Suddenly the whole mass of creatures moved forward, pouring down the hill like a river, with Ida Gripp leading the way.

"Are you ready, Mechanimals?" I cried to my troops. "Then let's go. *CHARGE!*"

We raced down the slope, but as we approached the oncoming hordes a hail of spinning clubs whizzed through the air towards us. A group of P.O.Ds were hit, and with a crackle of electric sparks they ground to a halt. It was not a good start, but the rest of us carried on and we were soon in the thick of Ida's invading army.

Mechanical Mayhem

BOOM! BASH! CRASH!

A battalion of Cronies attacked first, walloping my Mechanimals with their clubs. Steel-Skull picked the creatures up, one after another, and flung them away as if they were so many bits of rubbish.

"Go for it, Steel-Skull!" I cried above the noise, and my metal gorilla thumped his chest and roared.

Next came a wave of Horror Hounds. They raced towards the Armoured Armadillo, their eyes flashing and their jaws snapping like man traps. Luckily I had the Armadillo's remote control with me, and I quickly hit the "Fire" button.

BOOSH!

A great dollop of liquid blasted from the Armadillo's gunge gun, hitting the Hounds and turning them into living statues.

Still more Horror Hounds attacked, and a mechanical serpent fired a plume of fake flames at them. One of the Hounds grabbed the snake, there was a loud bang and it fizzled to a halt. My other serpents rattled across the ground, hissing and spitting their flickering lights, but a bunch of bouncing Cronies squashed them as flat as very flat pancakes.

Mad Dog joined in, racing around barking and snapping at everything in sight, but it was no good – we were gradually being overwhelmed.

"Come on, Mechanimals," I cried above the noise. "Don't give up now!"

From atop the Swamp Hopper, Fearless Freddie fired a net that caught twenty Cronies in one go, and my magnificent Steam-powered Rhino and Hydraulic Bison lowered their heads and charged, knocking the Horror Hounds aside and making a path straight through the enemy. That was more like it.

Jakeman's Patented Steam-powered Rhinoceros

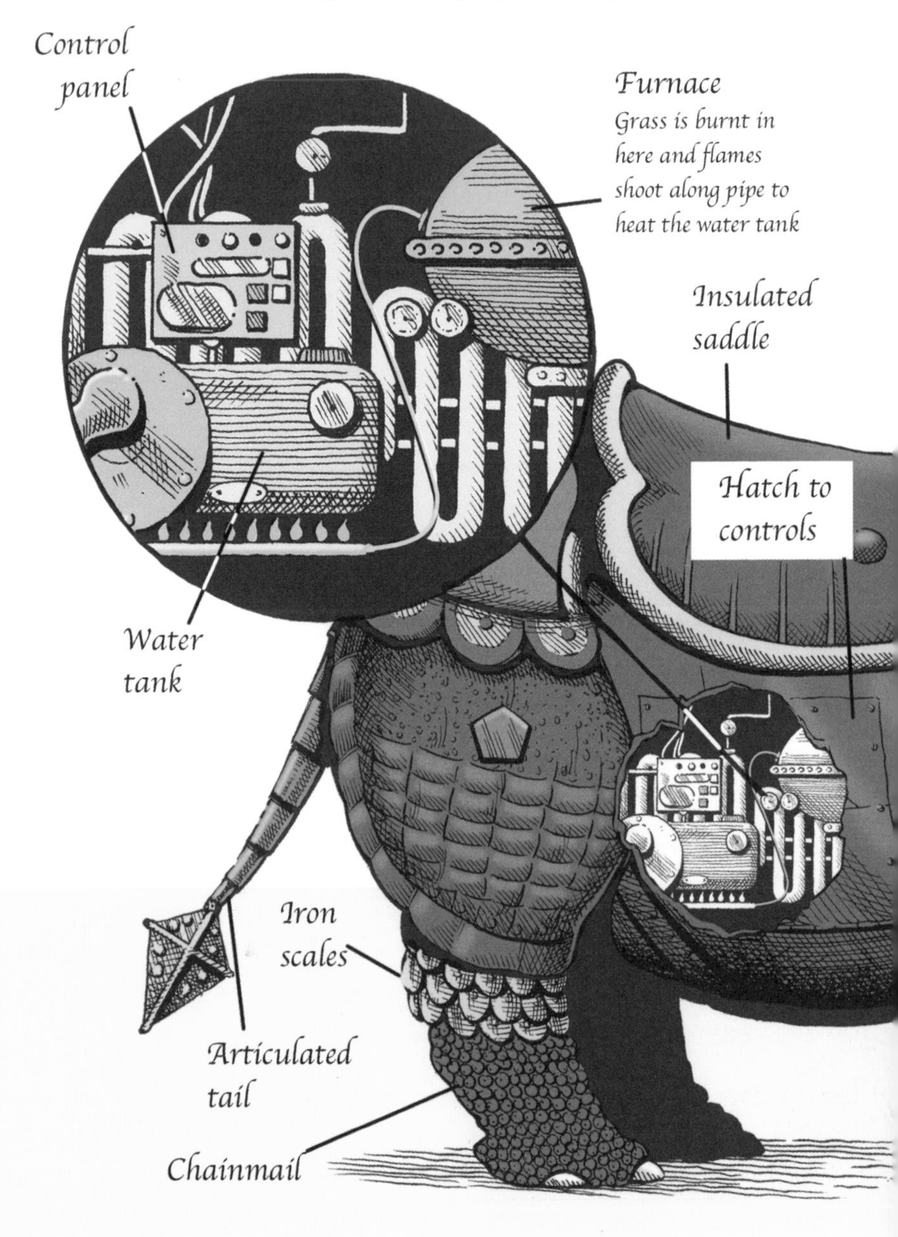

STATS:
Fuel: Dry grass
Ignition material: Flint
Max steam pressure: 1,000 kg/cm^2
Top speed: 35 kph
Weight: 5 metric tons
Ramming power: 6,000 kg/cm^2
Extra weapon: Thrashing tail

Patent No. 102633

Suddenly I heard a loud trumpeting noise and looked behind me. Princess Maya was riding towards us, high on Stompo's shoulders. She was followed by a crowd of jungle villagers leading a roaring Solar-powered Tiger. Amelia Bloop appeared on the Crocapotamus, and even my old school friend Titch turned up. He had squeezed his feet into the Hover Boots I had given him so many years ago and was swinging a discarded Cronie club.

"We got your S.O.S," yelled Amelia above the din. "Your Mechanimals saved us, now it's our turn to help you."

"Oh, brilliant! Thank you, so much," I cried as a spinning club whizzed past my head.

My friends charged into battle and were immediately set upon by a fresh battalion of bouncing Cronies. They were in danger of being instantly squished – but I had done my research and learned that Cronies couldn't resist anything sweet. So I had loaded my Scorpion's ammo compartment with big, sugary marshmallows.

As the Cronies tried to flatten my friends, I flicked a switch and a catapult emerged from the

Scorpion's back. A metal claw loaded the catapult with a marshmallow, pulled it back and fired – again and again and again.

The squishy sweets landed amongst the Cronies and stopped them in their tracks. They sniffed the marshmallows with quivering noses, and gave them a tentative lick. Then they fell upon the sticky goo, stuffing their mouths full, and they carried on stuffing them until they were terribly, terribly sick.

I drove the Scorpion through the mayhem, looking for Ida Gripp, and found her in the thick of battle. She was firing giant bee hairpins from her catapult at anything that came within range. Then she saw me, and a crazed look lit up her eyes. She raised the catapult and aimed it at me.

"I warned you, but you wouldn't listen would you, you irritating pest," she cackled above the din.

I pressed a button on the Scorpion's dashboard and two streams of powder sprayed out of its stings. I turned them left and right, spraying as wide an area as possible and hit Ida, the Cronies and the Horror Hounds all at the same time.

The powder's powerful itching ingredient immediately set to work and Ida dropped her catapult and began scratching furiously at her neck and arms and back.

"Aargh, it's torture! Make it stop!" she wailed like a siren.

Her troops were the same, scritching and scratching and wriggling and writhing. Some bounded off to jump in a nearby lake and soothe the terrible itching.

I fired the special launcher on my Scorpion. *Baboom!*

A long lasso shot through the air towards Ida. The loop dropped over her shoulders and the lasso's tail wrapped itself around and around her, tying her up in a tight cocoon.

"Let me go!" she screamed, struggling furiously as the last of her troops made a hasty retreat, chased by the Solar-powered Tiger.

The battle was over.

"We've won!" I cried, standing up in the Scorpion's seat and punching the air. "Thank you, everybody."

"It's the least we could do," said Amelia Bloop. "If you ever need us again, just send out your S.O.S sparrows, and we'll come running."

All my friends cheered and hooted and roared in agreement, and Stompo lifted his large metal trunk and gave a loud and triumphant trumpet.

A Problem Solved

Now I had caught Ida Gripp, what on earth was I going to do with her? I gave it some serious thought on the way back to my Factory of Inventions. I could ask her nicely not to attack us again, but I knew that wouldn't work. I couldn't keep her locked up in a cell – I would have to guard her forever more, and her Cronies would certainly try and rescue her. No, I needed a much better solution than that. And then I had it. I knew exactly what I would do with Ida Gripp.

As soon as we were back at the Factory, Steel-Skull and Fearless Freddie helped me roll one of my largest inventions into the yard – the miraculous **Gravitator**!

The Gravitator is a spaceship that flies by using Will Jakeman's Amazing Anti-Gravity Paint, a liquid I created quite by accident when I was mixing up chemicals in my lab.

When the Gravitator's "UP" lever is pulled, a network of nozzles sprays the outside of the spaceship with anti-gravity paint, and it rises into the air. It keeps on rising until another lever sprays detergent to wash the paint off. The spaceship is driven forward by a small propeller, powered by a simple, one-horsepower electric motor. It's a flying miracle!

The Gravitator

It's a Jakeman flying miracle!

PATENT PENDING

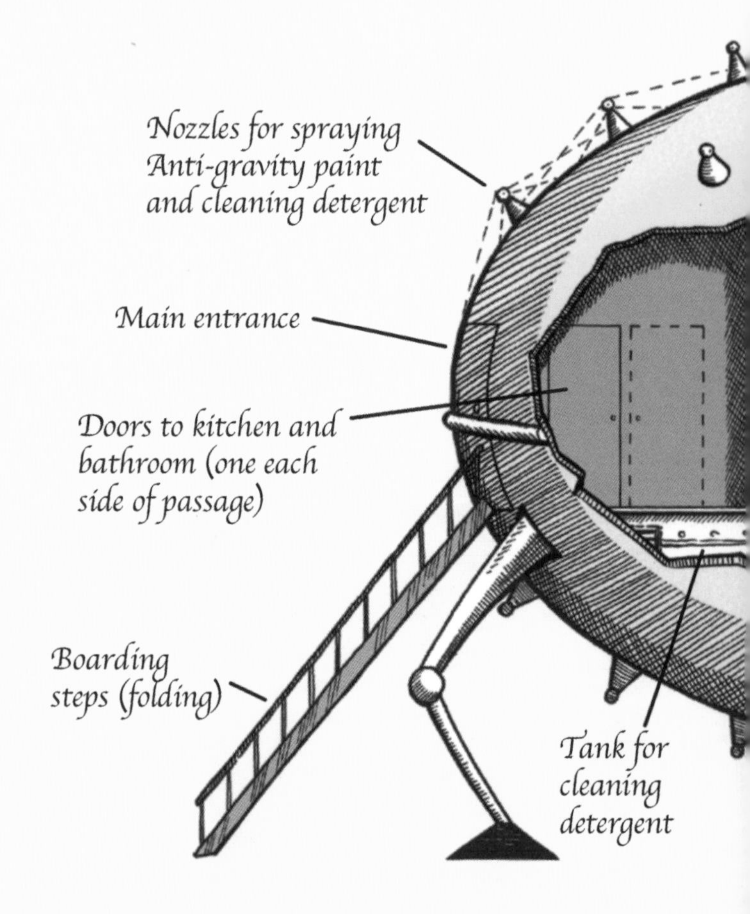

Jakeman has added millions of tiny crystals to his anti-gravity paint. These reflect the colour of the surrounding environment, making the Gravitator virtually invisible.

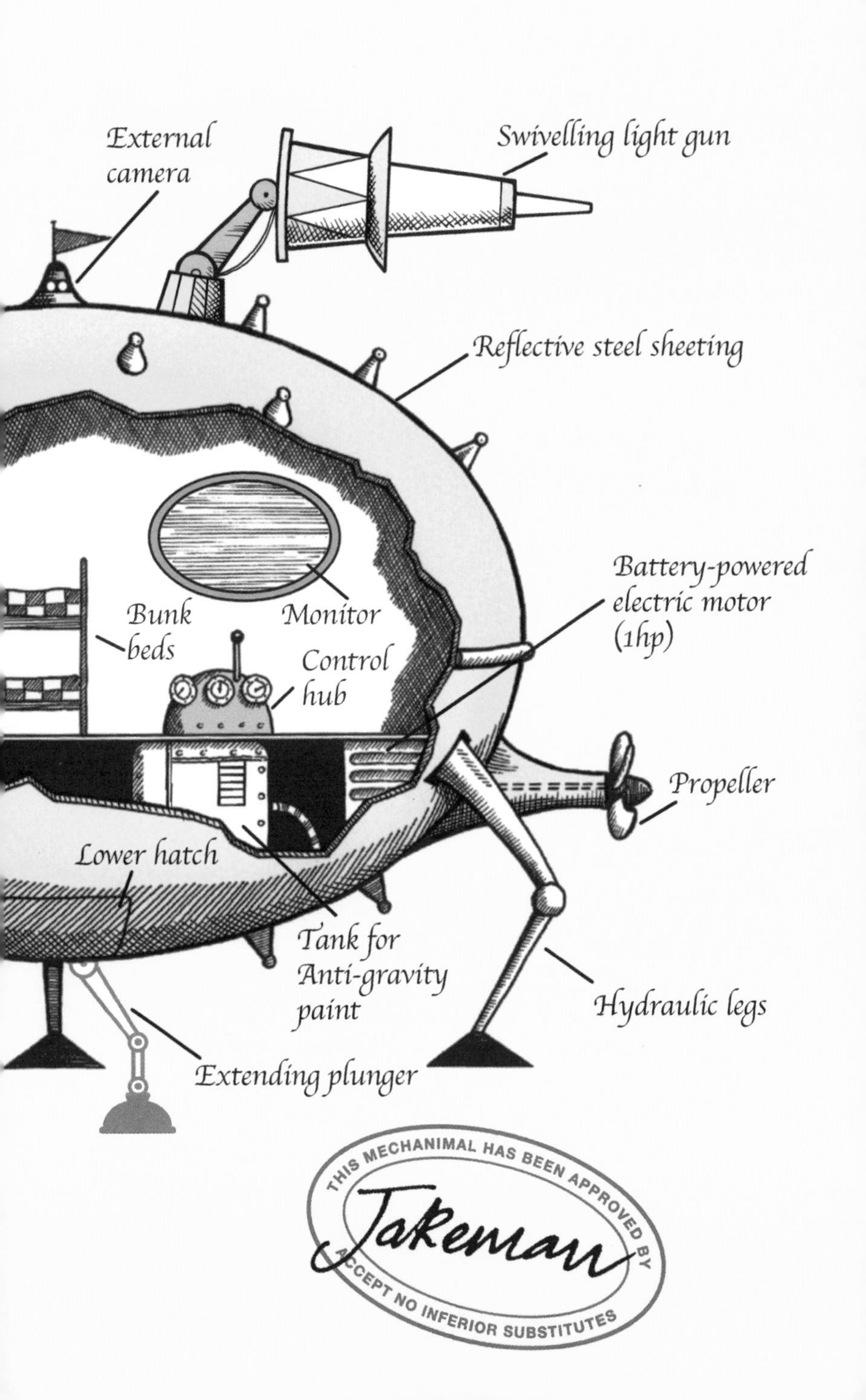
External camera
Swivelling light gun
Reflective steel sheeting
Battery-powered electric motor (1hp)
Monitor
Bunk beds
Control hub
Propeller
Lower hatch
Tank for Anti-gravity paint
Hydraulic legs
Extending plunger
THIS MECHANIMAL HAS BEEN APPROVED BY
Jakeman
ACCEPT NO INFERIOR SUBSTITUTES

Inside, the Gravitator has beds, a kitchen, a bathroom and a large supply of digital films to watch on the monitor. What better place to put Ida Gripp!

"Aaargh! Stop this itching, please," she begged again and again, as Steel-Skull carried her into the Gravitator and rolled her out of the coils of the lasso.

"You'd better wash it off. It's the only way to stop it," I said, pointing to the bathroom. Ida rushed in and slammed the door behind her. I waited until I could hear the sound of running water, then nipped into the main cabin and began punching a series of buttons on the control hub.

"OK, let's go!" I said to Steel-Skull, and we clattered down the steps, just as they began to slide up into the ship's fuselage. As we stood back, the nozzles began to spray Anti-gravity paint, and the Gravitator rose into the air. Higher and higher it went, disappearing beyond the clouds and out into space.

"Goodbye, Ida," I said, feeling relieved to see the back of my arch-enemy.

"Ughugh!" grunted Steel-Skull as he waved her goodbye.

I had pre-programmed the spaceship to go into orbit around Urf, and it would take Ida about two years to work out how to fly the Gravitator and bring it back home. There was plenty of dried food aboard, and lots of puzzle books and jigsaws to keep her amused.

By the time she gets back she might have learned a valuable lesson and become a better person, but we won't be seeing Ida Gripp for a long, long time – *and hooray for that!*

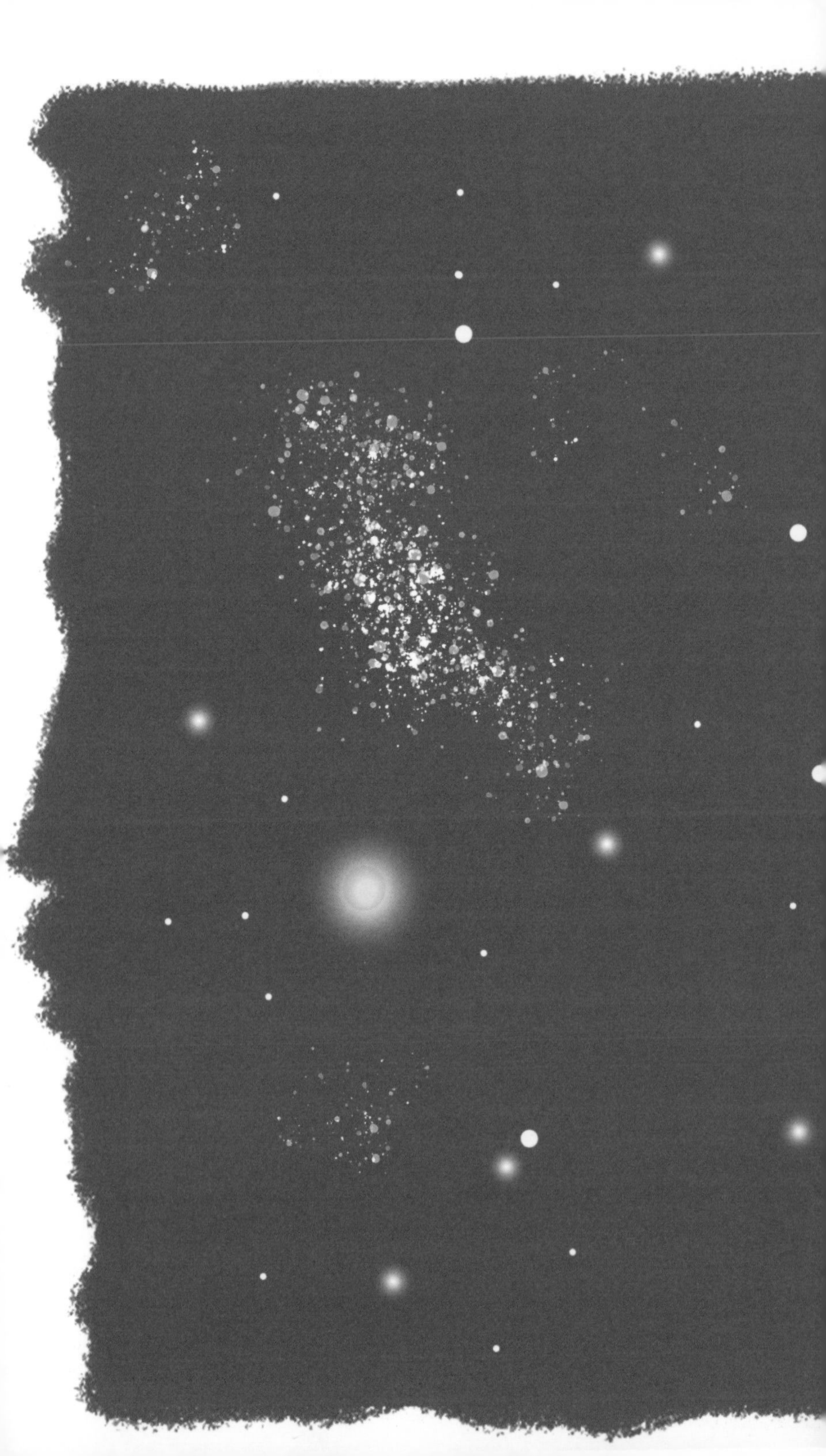

Hey, what's going on – where am I?

Cheerio, readers!

My name is Will Jakeman and I'm an inventor, perhaps the best inventor there has ever been, and I've created machines you simply would not believe!

Over the page you will find the Attack Shark that Fearless Freddie helped me build. It's designed to tackle any sea-going monsters, including the vile Vipersquid, that an adventurer might encounter. There is also my Scuttling Scorpion and the **Air-Rider**, a brilliant invention every child should own!

But I'm so old now I'm running out of ideas, and I could really do with some help!

So, how about you inventing a brilliant new Mechanimal for me? Draw your designs on the following pages, or better still on a separate sheet of paper.

Here are a few things to think about when you are inventing something:

1. What is it for?
2. What does it do?
3. What does it look like?
4. How does it go?

Who knows, one day you might have spectacular adventures with your very own marvellous Mechanimal.

Cheerio, good luck and watch out for Cronies!

JAKEMAN'S Hydroelectric

ATTACK SHARK

Fearless Freddie helped me build this Hydroelectric Attack Shark, a Mechanimal I designed especially for underwater explorers.

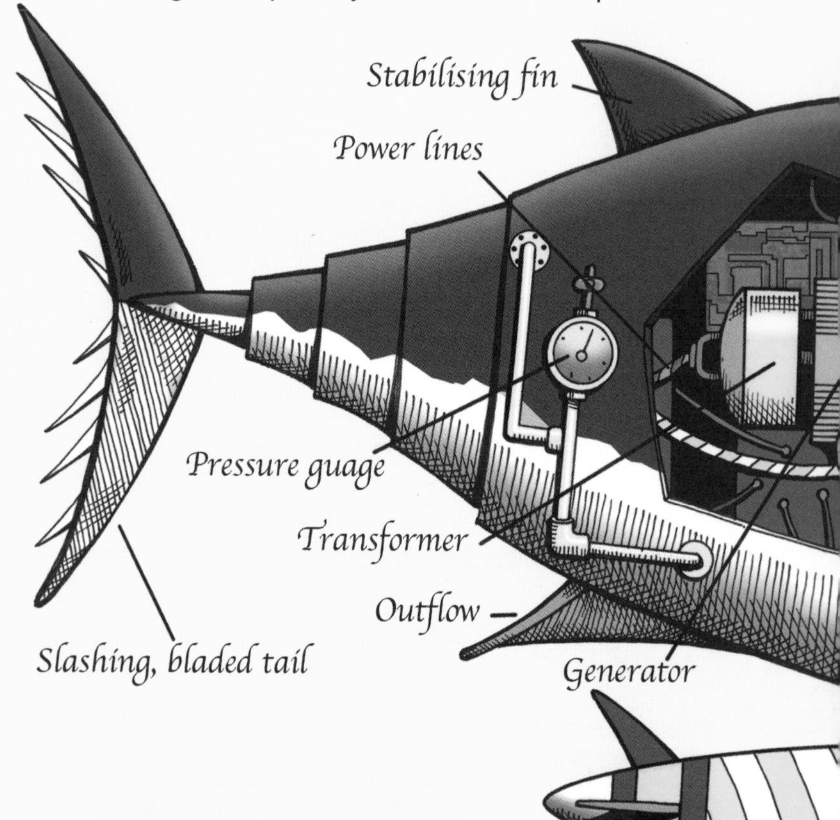

STATS:

Top speed: 50 knots
Bite force: 1,000 kg/cm^2
Chain saw: 3,000 rpm
Anti-Vipersquid factor: 10

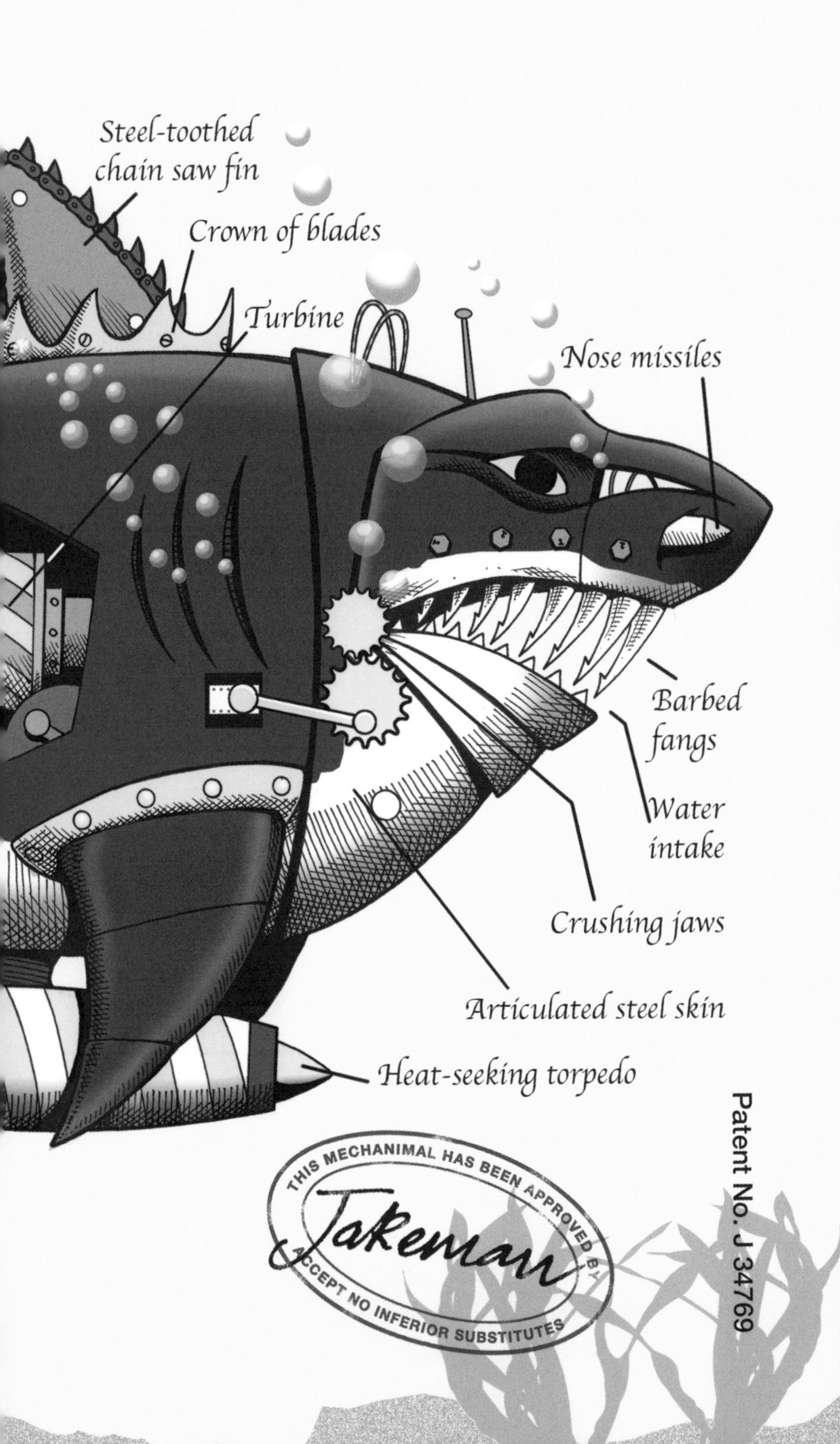
Steel-toothed chain saw fin
Crown of blades
Turbine
Nose missiles
Barbed fangs
Water intake
Crushing jaws
Articulated steel skin
Heat-seeking torpedo
THIS MECHANIMAL HAS BEEN APPROVED BY
Jakeman
ACCEPT NO INFERIOR SUBSTITUTES
Patent No. J 34769

Will Jakeman's Scuttling Scorpion

STATS:

Top speed: 40 kph
Side missile launcher range: 1 kilometre
Launcher can fire nets, flares or stun rockets
Catapult range: 200 metres
Claw pressure: 500 kg/cm^2

THIS MECHANIMAL HAS BEEN APPROVED BY
Jakeman
ACCEPT NO INFERIOR SUBSTITUTES

Driver's seat

Communications aerial

Loud speaker

Defensive snipping claws

Searchlight

Articulated joints

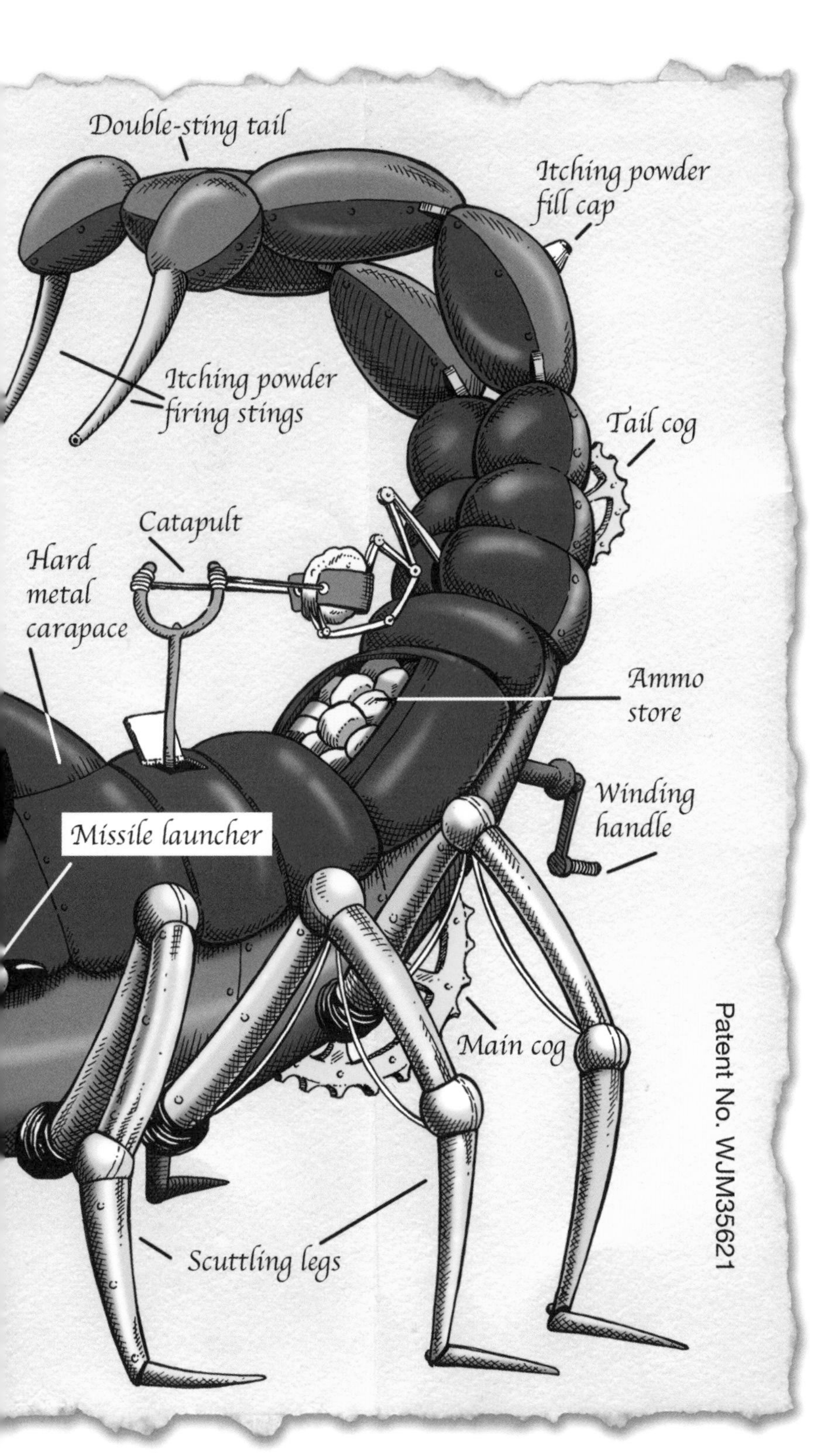
Double-sting tail
Itching powder fill cap
Itching powder firing stings
Tail cog
Catapult
Hard metal carapace
Ammo store
Winding handle
Missile launcher
Main cog
Scuttling legs
Patent No. WJM35621

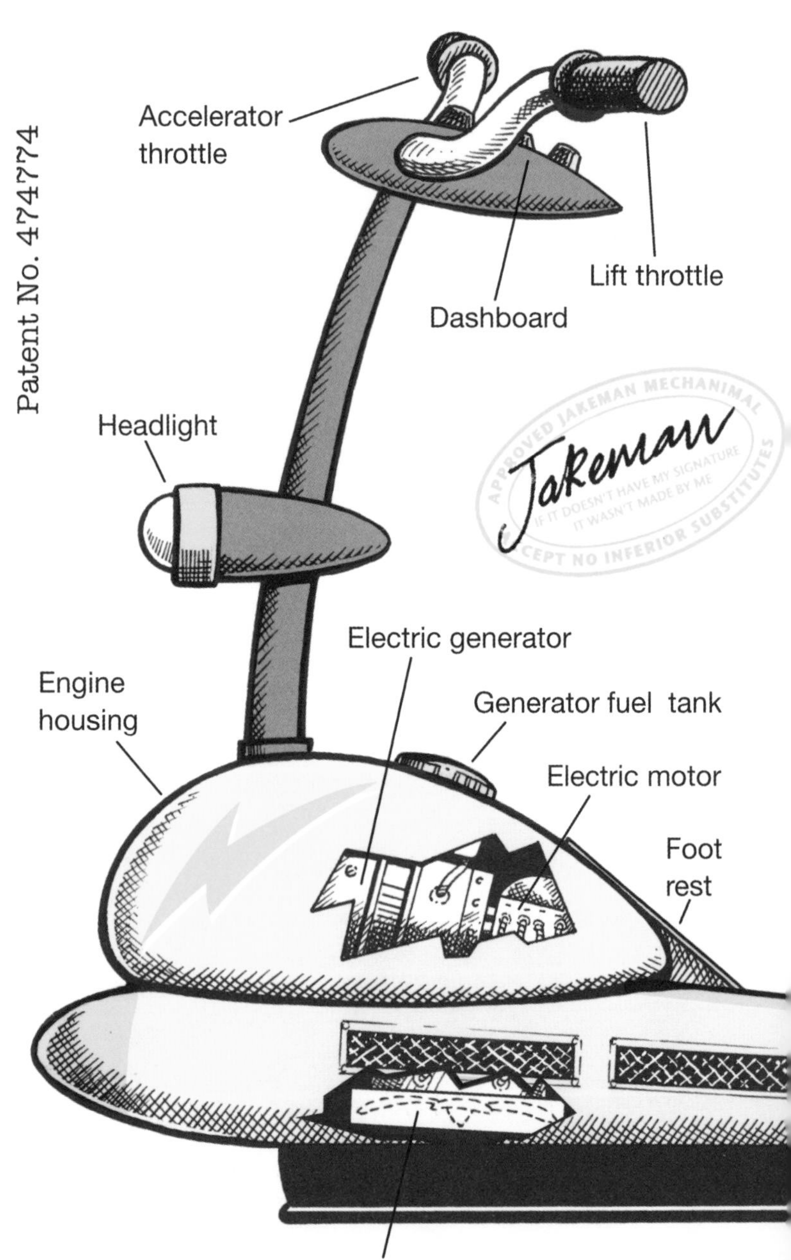
Patent No. 474774
Accelerator throttle
Lift throttle
Dashboard
Headlight
Jakeman
IF IT DOESN'T HAVE MY SIGNATURE
IT WASN'T MADE BY ME
Electric generator
Engine housing
Generator fuel tank
Electric motor
Foot rest
Series of powerful lifting fans sit in scooter's fuselage

Jakeman's Incredible

Air-rider

• Goes like a rocket!
• Goes on forever!
•Amaze your friends!
• Learn to hover, flip and spin!
• This is not a toy!

Mechanical Marvels For All Occasions!

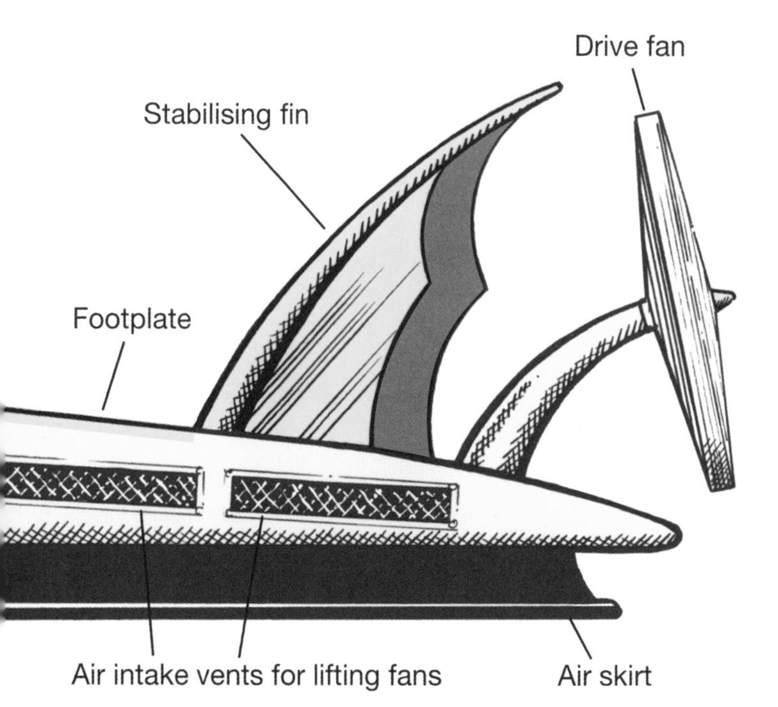

Inventor's name: ....

My invention is called: ....

....

I started this invention. Could you finish it for me?

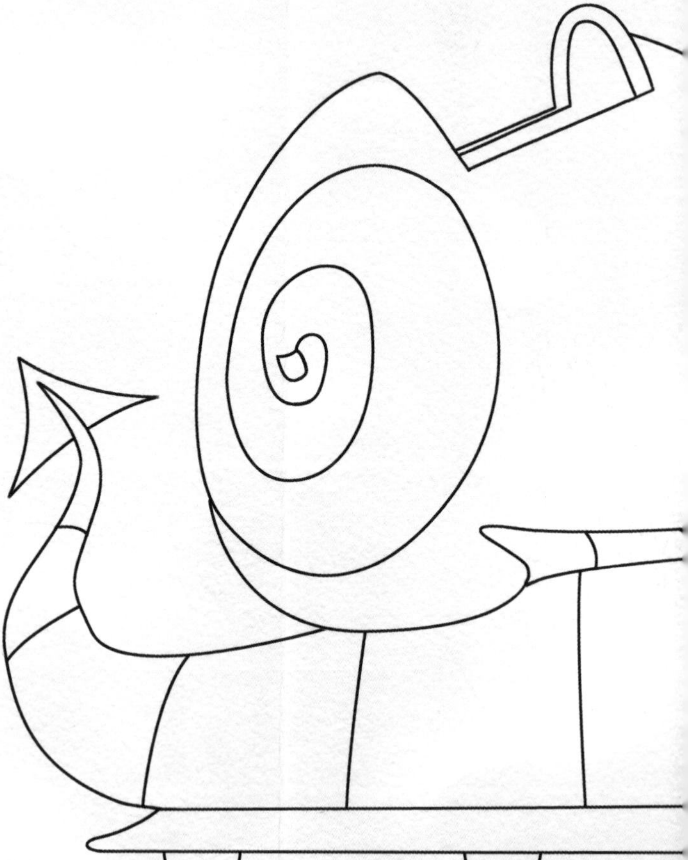

Here I've only drawn half a Mechanimal. Could you finish it for me? Don't forget to add lots of extras, and name all the parts, too!

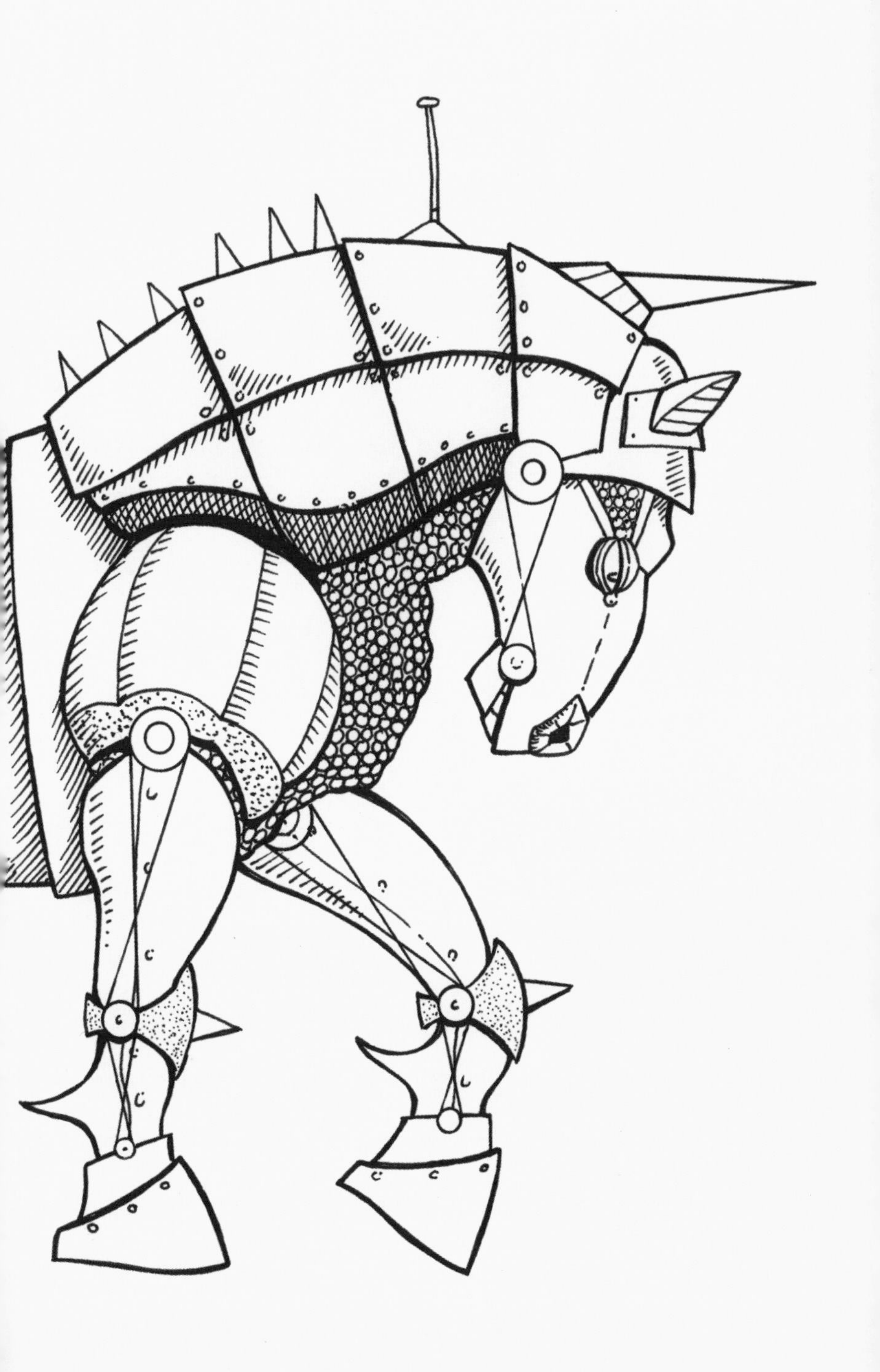

Inventor's name: ....

My invention is called: ....

....

And now, you're on your own!

Why not create your own Jakeman comic strip adventure, right here?

THE
END!

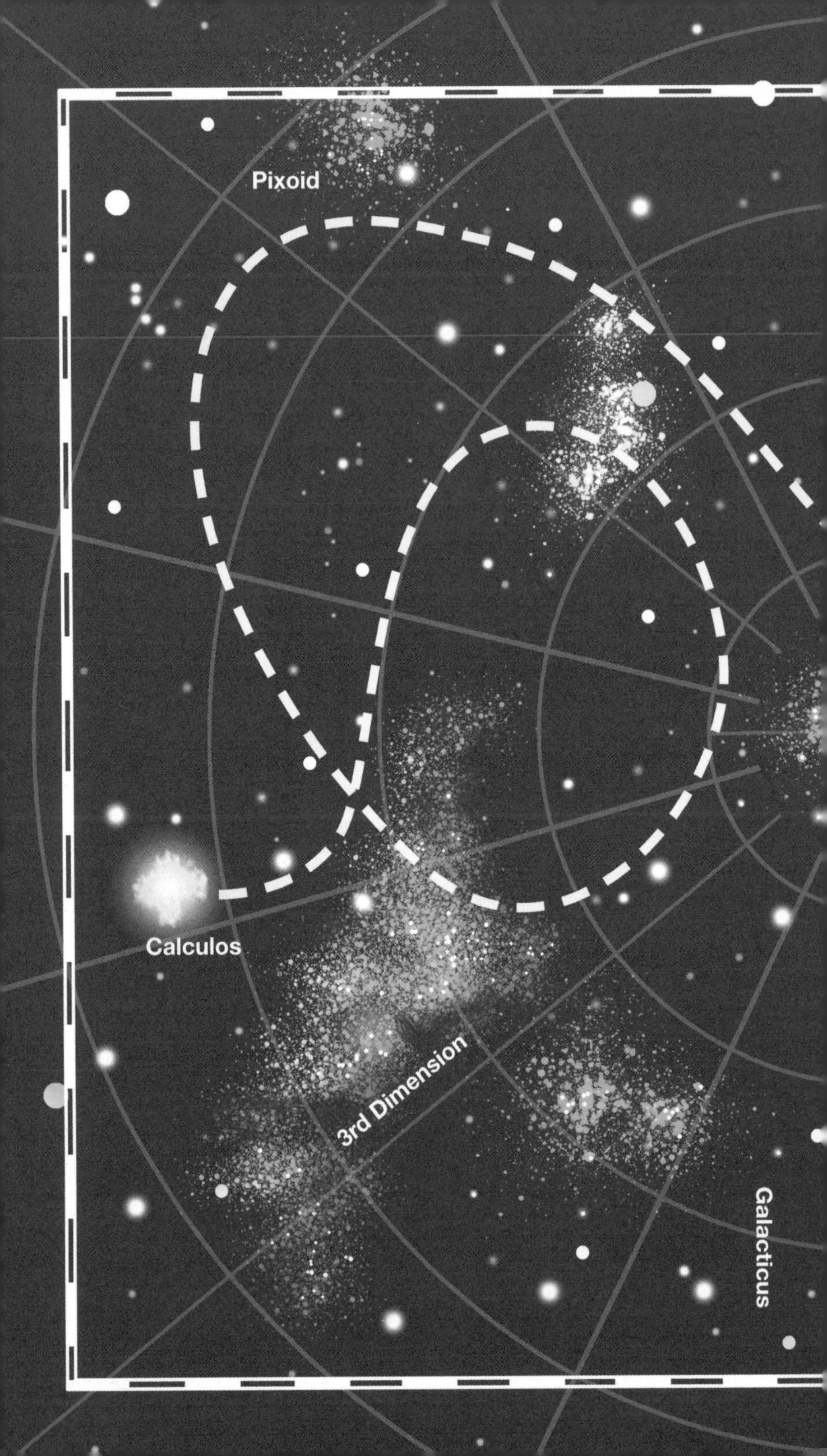

Pixoid

Calculos

3rd Dimension

Galacticus

5th Dimension
Argon
Zapta
Pavos

Nick Ward

A little bit about me

From the moment I read about Mole scribbling and scrabbling to the surface from his underground home in *The Wind in the Willows*, and followed Edmund through the fur coats hanging in a wardrobe that led to Narnia, I knew what I wanted to do – write and illustrate stories for children.

So I went to art college, and by the time I left I'd had my first book accepted for publication. I've been writing and illustrating stories ever since – picture books and story books and non-fiction books, too. I have written about a shark that cannot stop eating things, a fairy that can't help but be naughty and a robot superhero called Super Bot that lives on top of a skyscraper and saves people from a villainous toad.

I also became the Keeper of Charlie Small's journals. Charlie was only eight years old but lived for an amazing four hundred years – he wrote some diaries about his incredible adventures, packed with dangerous escapades, rotten rascals and tales of derring-do. One of Charlie's best friends was the amazing inventor, Will Jakeman. It was Jakeman's marvellous Mechanimals that helped save Charlie from certain disaster, time and time again. So as the Keeper of the Journals, I now have the honour to share Will Jakeman's very own story. If you liked this story, why not check out the Charlie Small books?